© Robert Boag Watson, 2023

All rights reserved

First published 2023

ISBN 9798865649748

The Velvet Guillotine

Written by R.B. Watson

1.

Academia is a complete waste of time.

Clarke Rossiter casually pushed open the door to the Playhouse, rubbing his eyes in a final unconvincing attempt to rid himself of the weariness that had plagued him throughout the last twenty - four hours, despite his concerted yet ultimately futile attempts to avoid it. He came in through the old brown door, one through which he had entered and exited countless times already throughout the course of his life, which was in its thirties, despite often feeling like it was entering its autumn rather than its mere spring. He looked around. It was Saturday night, but as he'd come straight from the 'office' and it was still relatively early, the great influx of paying customers had yet to arrive. Deciding to wait for a while to gauge the atmosphere and assess how he wanted the night to proceed, he ambled up to one of the many unoccupied stools, set his fatigued frame down and sat at the long mahogany bar.

It's only just after nine... probably still too early to be hittin' the hard stuff, was what he surmised after careful deliberation. The beer he ordered and subsequently drank was sufficient as a means of quenching his considerable thirst, and yet still somewhat disappointing as a kick-start to what promised to be yet another evening of debauchery. The barstool upon which he reposed did his backside no favours, such was its harsh, unforgiving nature. Pretty uncomfortable to say the least, but a few more beers or other weapons of (m)ass destruction would doubtless soften the blow somewhat...

     To many, the last week would have been fraught, stressful, infuriating even. But Rossiter's devil may care, playboy lifestyle meant that the events of the last seven days were little more than a spanner in the works, an inconvenience provoking only *mild* annoyance. The way she had treated him had surprised him, and he had been more than a little irked by the high and mighty, holier than thou tone which she had employed to address that final parting shot. But Clarke's relationship with the so called "fairer" sex was both a complex *and* remarkably simple one. To him, women were amazing, beautiful creatures that he simply loved to be in the company of. Less of a forbidden fruit, more one whose outer layers could be peeled off, opening the door to the sweet, succulent, almost intoxicating interior within, to be appreciated, savoured and devoured. He had long since ordained that there be no rules where women were concerned. He made no rules, neither did he choose to abide by any. In spite of his somewhat questionable life choices in the past, one thing was absolutely crystal clear in amongst the mayhem of this young man's mind; you make your own luck, and you make your own friends. It just so happened that bars, alcohol and beautiful women were Clarke Rossiter's chosen three...

     He leaned forward, placing his forearms on the sturdy mahogany bar, and subsequently ordered beer number two. One of the things he liked most about the Playhouse, his local bar of choice for nigh on ten years, was that there were almost as many different beers as there were women.

There was an ample array of both, and Rossiter appreciated the taste, texture and surprise factor of both beer *and* rear...

He sipped, and the amber nectar glided down his throat with refreshing ease. It had been a warm day but not stifling, as the oppressive, suffocating sweat fest of July and August had yet to hit. It was now late May, and soon would arrive his favourite time of the year; flirty, dirty, mini skirty...

As the ensuing minutes came and went, so did more beers. However, while the first one of this fraught evening had gone at least some way to quenching a thirst that was both literal *and* figurative, the ones that followed somehow failed to have the same effect. Rossiter found that he was no longer enjoying this somewhat sad charade of liquid companionship. The female presence wasn't up to much either, but it was still early. He decided to wait until 10:30pm – by now a mere twenty - seven minutes and probably another three beers away - and then assess the situation again.

As he swigged on his latest weapon of choice, his mind wandered to a place he probably didn't want it to... Charity. The way she'd treated him this afternoon and into the early part of the evening had been so typical of her! Clarke appreciated the fact that she was an ambitious, motivated and extremely passionate career woman. These were just three of a number of qualities that he had come to admire in her. Added to the fact that she also had everything he was looking for in purely physical terms, and you had the perfect components for either sixty years of happy marriage, or a recipe for disaster. It had to be said that for all her faults – of which there were many – Charity was certainly worthy of the name, when it suited her! She was very *giving* sexually. Not that Rossiter had, or would, ever *pay* for sex. Why would he ever part with cash for something that he could procure for free, and with ease? The way today's events had unfolded had been unfortunate, to say the least. But boys will be boys, and Rossiter felt no other explanation of his behaviour necessary. What they had was a purely 'casual arrangement', whatever *that* meant. And they were her words, not his. The fact that he was merely enjoying the company of yet another beautiful woman on his veritable *conne*-veyor belt of sexy sirens, without wanting to commit to anything serious (her words again), had caused her to take serious umbrage! Thus, they had argued. The details of said argument were unimportant. They always were, to him at least. Whenever these domestic disputes occurred, they were invariably instigated by her, not him. Rossiter saw no point in arguing with anyone, about anything. Differences of opinion were the way of the world and a part of life, often something that he believed should be embraced rather than being beguiled or seen as a source of conflict. But Charity was often impulsive, and sometimes irrational too. So the fact that she was capable of flying off the proverbial handle at any given opportunity was something that he'd come to expect from her. Maybe he even enjoyed her sudden outbursts, in some slightly perverse way. It has often been said that *charity begins at home*. Well, her bullshit certainly did.

    Rossiter looked around, keenly scanning the horizon to see whether anybody else had walked in through the Playhouse door. Whilst it was still relatively early in the proceedings, in Clarke's world at least, he noticed that more thirsty, devoted drinkers were indeed starting to enter the fray.

Come and join the party, ladies and gentlemen !
Almost *every* night was party night for this most enigmatic of men, and they were good parties, because *he* was invariably the one throwing them! Rossiter was the star of the show, and he and everybody else knew it.

In an age when modern society appeared to be degenerating into little more than a whirlwind of technology, tattoos and timidity, Rossiter felt that it was somehow becoming increasingly difficult to gauge where the world was heading, and whether it would even be a ride worth taking. He bemoaned the fact that in a world in which selfies were becoming more important than self-respect, where Tinder had triumphed over tender, and Whatsapp had usurped a simple *'hey, what's up?'*, the world was starting to lose any real sense of value. The ultimate irony was that in a modern world which was becoming increasingly inundated with technology, people were losing the ability (and sometimes even the *desire*) to *communicate* properly. In this 'modern' world of reality TV, the only reality that had any importance to Clarke Rossiter was his own. He preferred smart remarks over smartphones, he was more *don't give a damn* than Instagram. Snapchat? Fuck that. Sometimes he thought that maybe he was being a little too cynical in his criticism of this new generation's superficial whims. But Rossiter lived his life exactly how *he* wanted to, and he made absolutely no apologies for who he was, who he *chose* to be. In a world where flimsy feminism had begun to batter any semblance of real, raw masculinity into submission, Clarke was a *man*! Some might say a flawed one, but a man, nonetheless. He didn't want or *need* Facebook, its newsfeeds and phoney attempts to 'connect' the world. He just wanted friendly faces, real faces, and if they belonged to beautiful women, who was he to argue ?

The bar was getting busy now, but he was still yet to see any women that really appealed to him. He was potentially willing and able to have polite, intelligent conversation with all members of either sex. However, whenever he was really focused on having a big night out – and most of them were – Rossiter saw little point in interacting with people he didn't feel were worthy of his time. He wasn't arrogant, he merely knew his own self-worth. He had waltzed with whales, tangoed with trolls and been fellated by his fair share of fatties in the past. He deemed it part of the wonderful dance we call life. But those misdemeanours were behind him now, a distant memory of bygone, inexperienced days. He didn't necessarily want some kind of supermodel. Just a nice, genuine girl who he could share some good times with. But they had to be beautiful; that was non-negotiable. Rossiter believed that any true man worthy of the name ought to live by this virtue. Every man should at least *attempt* to get the kind of girl he wants, and screw everyone else, not least the lucky girl(s) in question. He felt that so many modern men merely settled for almost any girl that would have them, rather than going after the one(s) that they truly wanted. Another sad sign of these modern yet monotonous times...

He shuffled somewhat awkwardly on his barstool to engage the bartender. He was in discomfort rather than pain, as his right leg had been troubling him for the last few days, even with the aid of his cane. He almost toppled from his barstool in trying to adjust his weary frame, but said fear was allayed and he subsequently motioned over Beni, the voluptuous Playhouse barmaid who had initially been a mere server of drinks, but who had subsequently become a dear friend and confidante. She was in her mid fifties now, but you wouldn't have known it. Primarily because she had one of those faces which, although testament to a life not without its fair share of sadness, pain and suffering, nevertheless beamed happiness from its very core. Yes, Beni Rothwell had suffered at the hands of life's many trials and tribulations, and she recognised this. But Rossiter had always been amazed by how she managed to acknowledge that while life hadn't always been kind to her, she subsequently took it on the chin, maybe felt down for a while, but then always managed to brush herself off and get on with life. She was a warrior. A true fountain of inner strength and emotional fortitude. She had been of great help to Clarke in the past, and he was always conscious of that. Yes, Beni Rothwell had been through sad times, as had Clarke. But now, as she acknowledged his smile and wish to order another drink, she strode over to where he was sitting, with her trademark beaming smile and desire to entertain.

"Bonsoir, champion! How have you been? Not seen you around these parts for a couple of weeks! That's an eternity in Rossiter time!"

"Hi Beni! Yeah, not too bad. Just doin' my thing. The job's ok, but time drags when I'm stuck there all day! So I thought I'd come and say a hearty hello to my favourite buxom bartender!"

"Haha! Oh, Clarke! Always a pleasure to see you! What'll it be? As if I even need to ask..."

"I'm kinda fed up of beer! Gimme a Bourbon, neat. You know how I like it!"

Oh yes! She did know *just* how he liked it. After all, Beni was in the service industry, and as a bartender, she aimed to please. She'd been plying her trade at the Playhouse for just over five years now, and Rossiter had been the first customer through the door on her very first night, and had remained loyal ever since.

Beni's first night had been far from plain sailing! She was usually such an organised woman, but on that opening evening behind the fabled mahogany bar, she'd been all fingers and thumbs. A first shift that had bordered on disaster. She'd never really been able to ascertain whether her uncharacteristically clumsy performance had been because of nerves – she didn't *do* nerves as a general rule – or by virtue of the fact that she'd maybe been trying a little too hard to impress her new customers, especially the dark haired, handsome stranger who had walked in early that evening.

For nigh on five years they had been through so much together. Clarke had always been someone – especially at that particular time in his life – who had few friends, as he didn't feel that he needed allies or companionship. He ran his life the way *he* wanted to, and as a consequence, the way he conducted himself and chose to go about his business was down to him and himself alone. However, although he placed little credence in the importance of friendship, the ones he did have had been chosen very carefully, and hence they were extremely dear to him in many different ways. There was Greg Staton, his oldest friend who he'd met on his very first day of school when they were both just four years old.

Two young boys standing outside in the school yard on that first of numerous grey September mornings, feeling excited but also mildly apprehensive as they prepared to take their first cautious steps into the daunting world of academia. After they had been welcomed into the classroom by the teacher along with the rest of their new classmates, Greg and Clarke had chosen to sit together in an attempt to continue the discussion they'd begun just a few minutes earlier, only to be interrupted by the teacher, a supposed figure of authority. Since meeting on the first day of school, they had remained friends ever since.

     However, Clarke's friendship with Beni Rothwell was entirely different. When he'd first walked into the Playhouse on that balmy evening in late June, perspiring only slightly as a consequence of the fifteen-minute walk from the office and along the promenade, enjoying the early evening sun and admiring the scores of sexy, satisfied sunbathers determined to make the most of the day's final rays, the only thing on his mind had been a thirst - quenching beer. He would never have imagined forming such a significant friendship that evening, or even bothering to *talk* to a bartender. Especially one he felt was too old for him, and not his type. But converse they had. The initial chat hadn't been particularly mind-blowing or memorable in itself. The passing of time since that first interaction had meant that Clarke had forgotten much of what they'd talked about. He had vague recollections of the two new acquaintances having indulged in small talk, before he'd ordered a beer. Having just found out that it was Beni's very first night behind the bar, he had quizzed her about how to make various cocktails, before mocking her for being so nervous and subsequently offering to lend a hand in the making of Mojitos for the masses. Hence, they had joined forces in making scores of everyone's favourite mint-based tipple. And as they had got to know each other during the ensuing hours, with the conversation and drinks flowing freely, Beni's first night nerves had subsided as herself and Clarke embarked upon the first steps of their alcohol – based allegiance, and a lasting friendship had subsequently bloomed.

    Rossiter had left the Playhouse in the early hours, around 2:30am, after having assisted Ms. Rothwell in the customary closing time tasks of clearing away the masses of empty bottles and glasses that had been strewn across the scores of tables, occupied by the hordes of thirsty customers earlier in the evening. His recollections of that first ever closing time were somewhat vague. He seemed to recall there having been quite an array of beautiful ladies there that night. Women that would normally have tempted him to indulge in yet another round of his favourite hobby – seduction.

    Seducing women was easy for Rossiter. It always had been, or at least from his mid - twenties onwards, following a childhood and early adulthood that had proved testing on many levels, and for a number of different reasons. But he'd never really been able to pinpoint exactly why he'd become so skilled with the ladies as time had gone on. He was *relatively* handsome, one might say. But while the lord may have provided him with a reasonably strong hand in the looks department, the idea of him being the 'poster boy' for modern men would have been a misguided one. Rossiter wasn't the tallest, standing at only 5'10". He was in reasonable shape, courtesy of sporadic workout sessions at the local gym. However, it was fair to say that these visits had more to do with Clarke's enjoyment in checking out the girls' bodies on show, rather than working on his own chiselled torso. In any case, he didn't particularly enjoy working out, and had never really understood, even less adhered to, the view that being fit was necessary in the modern world. He somehow felt that society was becoming almost obsessed with being in shape, but he didn't go along with all that healthy body, healthy mind shit. Whilst he didn't disagree with the merits of being as physically healthy as possible, it seemed to him that people were becoming increasingly preoccupied with having (or at least trying to have) the perfect body, with toned rock-hard abs somehow being the benchmark for physical prowess. In much the same way that social media was seemingly disconnecting modern society from any sense of reality, Rossiter felt that people becoming increasingly obsessed with being perfect specimens was an indication of the narcissistic self-importance which was becoming so worryingly heeded by the youth of today.

 Hence, having put aside any thoughts of working out, and indeed beautiful women, he'd left the Playhouse that night. The interaction with Beni Rothwell had struck a chord with him. She was genuine, kind, fun, and *real*. He'd been able to work that out within a minute of having begun that initial conversation with her. She had no airs and graces. She had insecurities, a *killer* smile, and she (eventually) made amazing cocktails, thanks in no small part to Rossiter himself. So he decided that he would be back... he just hadn't realised at the time that it would have been quite so soon. But that, in essence, was the story of how he and Beni had met, back in the day.

Rossiter returned to the Playhouse regularly. It had long since become his favourite haunt. It was now Friday night, and he hoped the selection of beautiful ladies who would doubtless be in attendance would be worthy of his esteemed company.

He hadn't worked that day, or not as such, so he felt blessed with a freshness and zest that had been in relatively short supply in recent weeks, such were the stresses and strains of his ever increasing workload, coupled with yet another all too predictable bust-up with Charity only a matter of hours ago. She didn't really understand him. And sometimes, especially tonight, he thought it might be better that way. She was complicated. He was mildly stressed at the present time (although he never particularly let work matters affect him unduly), and he just didn't want or need any of Charity's aggravation on this particular night.

He set his tired behind down on one of the Playhouse's many barstools, and scanned the surroundings for his latest target. He wasn't feeling particularly fussy tonight. Just to be clear; he didn't fuck *every* time he ventured out. He didn't need to, and there were *some* instances – although rare - where he didn't particularly *want* to. Rossiter adored being in the company of women, the more beautiful the better. But all women held a special place in the heart of this most veritably virile of ladies' men. The more life went on, the more he had begun to realise that the ladies were a fine species. Every single one of them potentially had something inherently special and captivating about them; a flick of the hair, a seductive smile or a tempestuous glare, big boobs, smart moves and shiny shoes. All of these said attractions were a winning ticket in Clarke Rossiter's lottery.

He motioned Beni over:

"Hey Beni! How's it going? I reckon it's beer o'clock again!"

"Heeeeeeeeeey you! Looking thirsty tonight, Clarkey boy!"

"Haha! Too right!"

"So, what'll it be?"

"Just a beer for starters. Then I'll see how adventurous I get as the night unfolds..."

He gave her a sly, seductive wink, and turned around to look along the bar. *And there she was.*

A new, unfamiliar girl was standing a mere two or three yards to his right hand side. Her dark brown hair cascaded downwards, enveloping her lithe neck and falling just above the shoulders. Standing directly under one of the spotlights on the ceiling had caused the light to shimmer down upon those chocolate-coloured, undulating locks. She was leaning against the bar, supported by a slender right forearm, cradling a drink in her left hand. It looked like Malibu, but at that particular moment, her chosen tipple was the last thing on Rossiter's mind. He watched her as she took a first sip of her weapon of choice. The young lady was still side-on, so Clarke could only see her in profile. As such, this intriguing stranger's facial finesse had yet to captivate him. That soon changed, however, as her glass embarked upon the journey from hand to mouth and made first contact with those luscious lips. They were almost blood red, seemingly symbolic of both danger *and* eroticism. As Clarke knew only too well, such a combination was potentially fatal. Those lips were the forbidden fruit, and he knew instantly that he would never forgive himself if he didn't at least *attempt* to take a bite...

She wasn't very tall, a veritable *pocket rocket*. Her brown hair was swept away from the forehead to reveal beautiful blue / green eyes which shimmered like sunlight bouncing off a vast, emerald ocean. She was well-dressed too, wearing blue jeans and a red top to match the chosen shade of lipstick. In order to add a little more finesse to what was a predominantly casual choice of attire, she had opted on this particular evening for an elegant black jacket – he presumed suede – along with matching ankle boots which, like the rest of her, were classy yet understated, and therein lay her charm.

She reached forward again and sipped delicately from her glass. This brought a smile to Rossiter's lips, as he momentarily reflected upon many a pleasurable evening in the company of beautiful women. Cocktails such as the one being sipped by the new arrival seemed to be a popular choice for ladies of that age. She appeared quite young. Her choice of drink, the venues she apparently preferred to frequent, and the aura of innocent naivety that she exuded led him to surmise that she be around twenty-two or twenty-three. This assumption was subsequently made increasingly plausible by the as yet unknown stranger examining her phone at regular intervals. Quite *why* the younger generation felt the need to be contactable on a permanent basis had always been something of a mystery to Clarke. The seemingly constant necessity and desire to be in touch with the world by virtue of all its new, modern technology bemused him somewhat. Sure, Rossiter himself possessed a smartphone. But he only required it for occasional work-related matters, and for whenever a new girl whose contact details he desired came onto his radar.

No sooner had this thought entered his mind, than the Playhouse's newest arrival delved into her pocket to produce said phone. She took a few seconds to read and process whatever new information had been bestowed upon her, before the most *delicious* giggle left her mouth. Whatever she'd just read had clearly amused her, and a wry smile remained as she subsequently put the phone back into her pocket, before taking another sip of her drink.

It struck Clarke, that even her way of drinking was elegant. Whenever she sipped, she appeared to roll the beverage around that most enticing of mouths with sensual subtlety, before it duly descended into the throaty abyss, almost like a game of cat and mouse for the casual drinker. She was intriguing, she had begun to captivate him, and Rossiter wanted to play.

Placing her drink back upon the bar, little miss emerald eyes opened her mouth a few millimetres and the end of her tongue appeared, caressing her lips and licking away any remaining drops of drink. It was the simplest of acts, and commonplace in any bar around the world. However, it wasn't so much what she did, but the *way* in which she did it. The process only lasted a second or two. But it was seductive, sassy and savvy in equal measure. An act befitting its perpetrator, it seemed to Rossiter.

As this latest in a long line of fascinating females moved her head to scan the immediate surroundings, she turned and looked left. As her eyes met Rossiter's on that first, fabled occasion, she proceeded to once again lift her drink from atop its mahogany resting place, before raising her glass in his direction. This gesture was accompanied by a smile that simply screamed seduction, coupled with a teasing wink that seemed to suggest that she was inviting him into her world.

Clarke never felt uneasy or nervous, even when surrounded by the most beautiful of women. They were very much a part of his natural habitat. However, the sheer *power* of this intriguing, unknown newcomer's smile added an intensity to the situation that Rossiter was entirely unfamiliar with, and he had no idea why. He felt somewhat flustered, possibly even intimidated, by the incredible beauty of this miniature marvel standing before him. He had never experienced such feelings before, and they unsettled him, despite his attempts to subdue them. It seemed that the object of Rossiter's new found fascination was only too aware of his apparent unease. The acknowledgement of the effect her behaviour was having on the stranger standing to her left, caused a laugh to emerge from her mouth that combined amusement, intrigue, and a knowing self - assurance.

As Clarke continued to contemplate her, he was finding it increasingly difficult to look away. Her eyes sparkled, almost seeming to dance as she smiled. Hopefully she would be dancing to *his* tune before the night ended. But for that to happen, Rossiter needed to make a concerted effort to collect his thoughts, and embark upon his latest act of seduction in the tried and tested manner. He held out a strong right hand and introduced himself:

"Clarke Rossiter. A pleasure I'm sure!"

Despite feeling surprisingly outside of his comfort zone for one of the first times in his life, Rossiter hoped he'd somehow managed to quell the nerves and appear confident prior to, and during, the initial handshake. It was almost as though Clarke seemed to go into autopilot whenever he encountered a new girl. He never felt uneasy, and always gave a strong first impression befitting the attractive, immaculately attired, unshakably self-assured individual he believed himself to be. As his unexpected apprehension was beginning to subside, he collected his thoughts in preparation for the latest round of 'A' game seduction. It was a game he knew only too well and one in which his playing prowess was unrivalled – such encounters never held any surprises for him - and the moving from A to B and alcohol to bedroom always ran like clockwork. But just as he was about to find his rhythm, something happened to catch the lovable lothario off guard:

"I'm *not* so sure ! I never trust a man drinking bourbon *and* wearing a necktie!" She smirked as she held out her petite right hand to reciprocate the greeting gesture. "Analisse Lejeune. The pleasure's all *yours*…"

As the newly-befriended dynamite in denim regained her barstool and that most perfect of posteriors returned to its temporary home, the fuse had been lit, and she was about to blow him away…

2.

"So, Clarke... you've got exactly five minutes to dazzle me with this introduction. I'm hoping for - but not necessarily expecting - intrigue, amusement and who knows... *maybe* even a little bit of the extraordinary. Come on, let's see what you've got!"

And with that confident, bold, almost brash air of authority, the proverbial gauntlet had been well and truly laid down, the bar set tantalisingly high! Rossiter knew plenty about bars and getting laid... not to mention getting laid *in* bars, but right from those early exchanges, he sensed that this - and she – would present an entirely different kind of challenge, and it was one that Clarke was salivating at the prospect of.

As he proceeded to loosen his tie slightly in an attempt to make himself feel more at ease, he looked directly back at her. The majority of girls he hit on in bars and other such venues were little more than tools for his own amusement, a source of entertainment in the mere passing of time. Another notch on the bedpost, another *conne-quest* to feed his ego. However, as he contemplated her once more, looking straight across and making sure to use that strong, direct eye contact for which he was renowned - just one of his many secret weapons - he felt a strange mixture of intimidation *and* comfort. He had often heard it said that the eyes were the window to the soul. But his famed, powerful eye contact had so often served as a vehicle to grant Rossiter entry through countless other, altogether more intriguing and appetising windows. He'd often smirked when reading futile internet advice and throwaway nonsense in dating books deigning that maintenance of eye contact was a sign of confidence. In Rossiter's eyes (pun intended), confidence in and of itself meant very little. As he was growing up, first as a teenager and then as a young twenty-something to whom the term *adult* barely deserved to be attributed, such was his naivety in the exuberance of youth, he along with countless other youngsters of his generation had been given dating advice such as *show confidence*, or *just be yourself*, and other such pearls of wisdom proffered by well-meaning but ultimately mistaken parents and peers. Confidence wasn't and isn't something that you can just naturally *show*, exhibit, exude. If a kid is naturally shy, withdrawn and lacking in self-assurance, advising the young man to just somehow, magically *be confident* will prove utterly pointless. As for *just being yourself*... well... if that *self* has never been good with women, why would parents ever assume that maintaining the status quo, doing exactly the same things and getting exactly the same results – namely zero success with the opposite sex – would bear any fruit? Such advice was often well-intended, but it rarely - if ever - worked. Rossiter had learnt this the hard way, enduring a childhood and early adulthood with almost no success or affection bestowed upon him by girls at school and university, let alone sex.

    Like so many young men growing up at the same time as him, the general advice he'd been given had been severely lacking. It was ironic that then, and still now, young men needed sound advice and a solid foundation upon entering what is, in many ways, a man's world. But where were the strong, savvy, self-assured male role models to impart this knowledge and provide such a foundation? Rossiter bemoaned the fact that many modern men were being emasculated by women heralding the virtues of modern-day feminism, jumping on the delusional bandwagon of self-importance and running over any sappy, self-deprecating excuse for a man who stumbled into its (and their) path.

The professor had learnt tough lessons about women, and about life in general. The fact that he'd struggled in his early years had forced him to find out the hard way and set off upon his journey of self-improvement. It appeared that the next step of said journey was to be taken right here in the Playhouse, right now...

Best foot forward, Clarkey boy!

"Well, miss Lejeune... before I endeavour to regale you with an insight into myself and my veritable mundo of mayhem, I want to ask *you* a question! After all, we've only just met. And while I will make no attempt to hide my delight at this chance encounter, I need to find out more about you and your feminine wiles before deciding whether or not to unburden and un-bourbon myself to you. You said you never trust a man wearing a tie! Well, I also tend to have reservations about ladies drinking cocktails so early in the proceedings. Dazzling eyes and exotic-sounding names merely cause my scepticism to skyrocket! French, I presume...?"

The slightly startled and also mildly amused look in Analisse's eyes gave cause to suggest that she hadn't been expecting such a riposte from the unknown newcomer. And yet, there was also a sense of anticipation, a hunger and desire to find out more. Who did this guy think he was, bombarding her with a barrage of highly-strung hyperbole? His response had taken her by surprise, although she had to admit she immediately found him entertaining, with such a tantalising turn of phrase, too. Quite the wordsmith, it would seem!

Clarke shuffled on his barstool, quickly looking around to survey the scene once more. The Playhouse was starting to fill up as the night progressed. But he wasn't particularly interested in anything – or indeed *anyone* – in the vicinity at that particular point in time. The Frenchy was beginning to intrigue him, and he had a sense that the feeling was mutual. Whereas only a matter of minutes ago, she had seemed distracted, at the mercy of her phone and even slightly bored, now she had altered her posture, turning to face him directly, to ensure that the initial conversation could continue.

She sipped slowly and intently on her drink, looking around to take in the surroundings, her eyes darting left and right, perhaps a little bit nervously, before settling once more upon the not unattractive face before her. She seemed somewhat unsettled, for whatever reason...

"You certainly seem to have a way with words, Mr. Rossiter! But why should I *believe* any of them? I mean, sure, guys come in here every weekend, hell even every night of the week, to have a drink or two, pass the time, hit on girls in an attempt to "get lucky". Don't get me wrong; you seem like an intriguing character, and I'm always open to meeting new people and having fun. But men like you are ten to the proverbial penny... and words are just words... although first impressions would suggest that *yours* are more entertaining than most uttered by the usual deadbeats that walk through these doors. Congratulations! You've peaked my interest! You've just earned yourself an extra few minutes..."

She took another sip, before placing her drink back down on the bar. As she did so, Rossiter felt a strange sense of accomplishment at having smooth-talked his way into a promising conversation with the newcomer, coupled with an uneasy feeling. A sensation that as yet, he couldn't quite place. Couldn't quite put his proverbial 'magic' finger on...

"Please excuse me, Mr. Rossiter. I'll be back shortly..."
And with that, she descended from the barstool, dismounting with a swift elegance that left Clarke smirking in spite of himself as she neglected her drink, making for the Playhouse bathroom.

The bar was rapidly filling up, and as Rossiter watched the young lady make her way to use the facilities, he couldn't help noticing that she, like himself, walked with a slight limp...

3.

The shrill, piercing sound of the 07:30 alarm was loud enough to wake the dead, and even Rossiter. Whether the dead ever *got* hangovers was a matter he would doubtless contemplate over his morning coffee, which at this point he felt may be his best hope of staying alive on this most difficult of get - ups. Maybe that was what heaven was like; a utopia free of hangovers and early morning starts.

He gave his thick head a quick shake, slapping his tired face to get rid of the cobwebs, before dragging a heavy hand through his bedraggled hair in an attempt to eliminate the unwelcome Friday fatigue. Indeed, it was Friday, but the weekend being just one more working day away was of little comfort to Clarke as he proceeded to drag his booze - addled body from the comfort of his bed.

As he stumbled sleepily into the bathroom to pee, he leaned against the toilet bowl and looked into the mirror hanging on the opposite wall.

Jesus, you're lookin' old, Rossiter! Thirty goin' on sixty!

The sound of piss hitting porcelain startled him out of his befuddled reverie, accompanied by a loud, rasping fart. He yawned, stretched his arms upwards as if in celebration of the crescendo of noise having subsided, then finished pissing, took a quick shower, and headed into the kitchen to make coffee.

He sat for around twenty minutes, sufficient time to drink his coffee and devour a plate of scrambled eggs. His favourite hot beverage was a longstanding morning ritual... battles with eggshells and frying pans less so. But the onset of yet another hangover had forced his hand somewhat, dictating that he should eat something, no matter how unsubstantial, in an attempt to soak up last night's booze before heading off to work. In fact, today's *gueule de bois* was something of a mystery to Rossiter. He had partaken of a beer while watching the football, followed by a couple of whiskies as he worked on his latest writing project. But all things considered, the previous evening's alcohol intake hadn't been particularly excessive; not to Clarke, at least. He'd briefly contemplated returning to the Playhouse, before instead opting to stay at home and concentrate on his scribbling. He also had a considerable amount of preparation to do before the new academic year started, so he'd decided that the Playhouse would have to wait for another night. Tonight.

  In the meantime, today he needed to focus. Classes at Congletown University weren't due to start again for another couple of weeks. However, such was the amount of planning and organisation required prior to the first day of the semester, that these next few days promised to be stressful, aggravating and doubtless energy – sapping.

He enjoyed his job, not least the scores of new twenty - somethings in tight tops and other equally revealing attire embarking upon their first fruitful forays into higher education, but to say he loved his profession - sexy new students aside - might have been stretching things somewhat.

  He glanced quickly at his watch, feeling slightly agitated that it was already 08:05, picked up his briefcase and navy blazer from off the table in the hallway, and exited through the front door. One of the advantages of not driving was that it negated any problems owing to the swathes of morning traffic in these parts. His walk to work gave Clarke the opportunity to blow away any final remnants of morning fatigue, whilst also providing him with the chance to think, and exercise into the bargain. Although the physical effort of walking at such an early hour on an almost daily basis (he also taxied to work occasionally, given that two of his friends, Vincent and his son Bert, ran a cab firm), wasn't always welcome, especially given that his right leg had been troubling him even more than usual of late, he was grateful for the fresh air, and the chance that the 15 - minute perambulation gave him to ruminate upon what the coming day may have in store, and a multitude of other things besides.

He felt especially fatigued today, and the hangover didn't help, but as he approached the university building with its once imposing but now strangely homely huge white iron gates rolling into view over that oh so familiar of horizons, his brain kicked into gear. As he entered through the gates and made his way up the steps into the building towards his office, the tiredness subsided, and he was ready to go. Another day, another scholar!

The walk from the entrance to his office ordinarily took little over a minute, as he headed down the main corridor past the Dean and Deputy's offices, before turning left onto a second walkway towards his office. This part of the building incorporated an intricate series of corridors panelled with dark wood, giving an impression of prestige without pretension; Congletown University's wish was to showcase its academic excellence without bordering on the ostentatious.

Rossiter withdrew the office key from his trouser pocket. As the door – whose classy black and white plaque adorned with his name in elegant golden writing – swung open, the master was entirely at home in his quarters. Professor C. Rossiter was ready to go.

Setting his briefcase down upon the desk, he surveyed the room. A thin but nonetheless noticeable film of dust layered the cedar bookcases which adorned three of his office's four sides. He'd thought about purchasing a fourth to add even more books to his *shell of shelves,* but had subsequently decided against doing so, esteeming that lining volumes along all four walls would border on the pretentious, even for a reputable academic such as himself. Instead, he had opted to make the final wall in the large, rectangular room home to photos of his family, friends and favourite football team, all so cherished by Rossiter for different reasons. As he strode over to admire one of said frames adorning the opposite wall, a large reprint of his beloved football club's crest, a metre high and sixty centimetres wide, and bearing the club colours of black and white with just a subtle hint of gold, he saw as he approached that a thin veil of dust remained atop the picture frame, akin to that that he had seen on the bookshelves upon entering the office. He surmised that the cleaner – incidentally named Fina – had yet to do her morning rounds. Today was to be her first day back following a few days off, the layers of dust and residue testimony to the short period of neglect where polish had not had cause to meet with wood. It was now approaching 08:40am, a mere twenty minutes before Tunisian – born Fina was due to make her daily appearance in these hallowed halls.

This was Rossiter's second year teaching at Congletown, and Fina had in fact started on that same balmy, mid September day. He'd remembered her looking flustered, nervous and perhaps even mildly irritated as she'd forced her way through the main doors in a fashion akin to a power walk, before angling a piercing look in Clarke's direction that was irate, bristling with nerves, and almost resembling a glare... the reason for which he hadn't at first been able to ascertain. However, in spite of her having initially seemed cold, distant and wary, subsequent interactions with Fina revealed that her reluctance to engage and interact around the workplace, not only with Clarke but also with other staff members, acted as a kind of shield. Fina later recounted that she had been born into an extremely impoverished family in one of Tunis' most dangerous and disadvantaged neighbourhoods, and that as such, her mantra was that she had been brought up to appreciate the value not only of the material possessions that she'd never been fortunate enough to acquire, but also of the values of honesty, integrity, and hard work. Fina was not a cold person, quite the opposite in fact, once you got to know her. Her decision to maintain a certain distance, particularly during *early* exchanges with new people, was merely a way for her to protect herself and continue to adopt the values that had served her so well during difficult times in her teens and an often equally fraught adulthood.

Just as Rossiter reminisced about that first ever meeting with *Fina the cleaner*, the office door opened with a firm pull of the handle, and in she glided.

"Morning, Clarke!"

"Hi Fina! How are you this morning? Ready to embrace the calm before the storm?"

"Haha. Yes indeed. I'm raring to go! This office isn't going to clean itself."

"Right you are! I'll let you get settled. Coffee's on the way!"

"Thanks! Make mine extra strong this morning please, if you would..." With that, she forced an agitated half smile and exhaled, puffing out her slightly rosy cheeks. She appeared tense; Rossiter had picked up on that as soon as she had entered the office mere seconds earlier. The ensuing coffee break would doubtless provide an opportunity for him to ascertain exactly why:

"It's the *boy*, Clarke. Getting him to school, hell, even dragging his lazy behind out of *bed* in the morning is getting more and more difficult with every passing day. And even when he *does* go, it's almost as if he hadn't bothered! No ambition, no enthusiasm, no application or hard work. These are the values I was raised with. But not the boy. He needs to pull his head out of his arse, work hard and stop messing about at school! It's starting to cause even more friction between his father and I. Things are tense at home, and I'm tired. Put it this way, I'm glad to be here working, surrounded by people with some degree of intellect, integrity and sanity!" *She needed that coffee...*

The subsequent break followed much the same path as the usual morning pleasantries, with Clarke still jaded from a rare early start and the ensuing walk to work, and Fina bemoaning her hardships at home. Her husband was, by all accounts, a difficult man; dominant, controlling, and

(Rossiter suspected) handy with his fists when the mood took him. However, for as much as Congletown's most respected, qualified and revered, if sometimes somewhat controversial professor liked his cleaning colleague, their relationship had always been friendly, yet purely professional.

Rossiter finished his coffee, which was by now luke warm, and edged out of the office to attend to a few of the more 'urgent' bits of paperwork. He subsequently spent the rest of the morning attending to the usual plethora of mundane administrative tasks – as was always the case whenever a new academic year approached – before rapidly partaking of a most average of sandwiches at around 1pm, and heading home again soon thereafter.

The walk home in the early afternoon sunshine was the same as always. September was an enjoyable month; still nice and warm, but not the oppressive, stifling heat that always hit these parts in the height of summer. Walking down the promenade and looking out over the water, Clarke spotted a couple of cuties taking the time to catch a few late summer rays, to top up their tans and make one final concerted effort to work on their beach bodies, before confining their bikinis to the bedroom drawer for another year.

He crossed the street and headed up the driveway, quickly checking the letterbox to ascertain that there be no newly deposited mail. Empty. Having succeeded in completing all of the necessary paperwork and preparation during what had proved to be a surprisingly productive morning, his schedule was now free to take a nap, and motivate himself for tonight's return to the Playhouse. It hadn't been long since his last visit, but he felt in the mood for some fun tonight. One of the reasons he loved it so much there, was that despite its familiarity, there were often surprises in store...

He took a rare look at his phone, saw no new messages (or none of *note*, at least) and decided to message Beni the barmaid:

Hi Beni! It's been a while! Working tonight? I may swing by!

Her response was almost immediate:

Clarke! Always a pleasure! Yeah, I'm in tonight from 9pm until closing. There'll be a free bourbon with your name on it!

So, that was settled. He'd probably head down there at around eleven. To go too early was pointless, due to the lack of women. He hung up his jacket in the hall, put his briefcase back in its resting place, and went to lie down.

  He awoke at around 7 pm, much later than he'd planned to, doubtless as a consequence of the previous few days' drinking exploits catching up with him, coupled with this morning's preparation for the beginning of the new academic year. He had a quick shower to freshen up, and then sidled into the kitchen to pour a glass of white wine before heading out onto the terrace (or the *bandstand*, as his father liked to call it), and sitting down to enjoy the late summer sunshine. Rossiter enjoyed these evenings outside. Neither his apartment nor the adjoining terrace were particularly big, but just big enough for him, and secluded, too. For as much as Clarke loved going out and socialising – particularly with members of the opposite sex – he also enjoyed some degree of solitude when at home. It gave him the opportunity to get some much needed *down time*, to coin a terrible American expression - an increasing number of which were creeping into British English - and it was a trend he despised. But nonetheless, his time at home or on the balcony allowed him to relax, read, write, eat and drink.

As thoughts of liquid refreshment entered his head once more, he rose from his patio chair and sought glass of vino number two from the fridge. Rossiter wasn't an alcoholic, but it would be fair to say that he indulged rather more than he ought to in the demon drink at times. His vices were the usual ones, especially for young men of his age; a good drink, women, and the occasional Cuban cigar. He doubtless over - indulged at times; but Rossiter loved his life, and made absolutely no apologies for it. He intended to be here for a good time, not a long time. That was the mantra he chose to live by, and it had served him well so far.

Sipping on his latest glass of wine, he scanned his phone to decide whether to reply to Charity's message from earlier in the day. An accountant by trade, she was a serious career woman who worked extremely hard, and appeared to be a great professional. But she was beginning to bore him, and was also incredibly high maintenance. Drama was never too far away where she was concerned, coupled with regular mood swings and the frankly ridiculous demands she placed upon Rossiter – or any man (or woman) she chose to date for that matter – she was way too much hard work! Clarke had attempted to clarify right from the start, that he would only ever be interested in occasional get - togethers (read drinking and sex) and absolutely nothing more. He didn't want or need the drama from Charity – or any other woman for that matter – but his early attempts to explain this had fallen on deaf ears. If today's latest message was any indication, they continued to do so. He had been direct, maybe even a little abrupt, but nevertheless totally honest with her. He would never be held accountable to her – a fucking accountant, no less – she was just too much of a drama queen. He glanced one last time at the message, deleted it, and duly erased her number from his phone. He wasn't a charity case... especially not now. Next!

    Having finished his drink, he picked up his jacket from the hallway and slung it nonchalantly over his shoulder, before taking one last look at himself in the mirror, running a hand through his freshly washed hair, and striding purposefully out of the front door. The walk to the Playhouse, which was now so familiar to him, took around twenty minutes. As he approached, he felt confidence pulsing through his body. He always enjoyed going there – it had become by far his favourite bar – but tonight he felt a sense of anticipation. It was as though tonight, something was about to happen. He couldn't put his finger on it, but he was unable to shake the feeling that tonight would be memorable. He just didn't know *why* yet...

    He pushed back that oh so familiar of doors, scanned the surroundings, and took his place on a barstool, ready for the fun to start. Rossiter always selected a seat in as central a position as possible at the bar. This not only potentially gave him more space, but it also provided him with the opportunity to speak to as many people (read *women*) as possible, both on his left and right hand side. A central vantage point was the most practical for him to seek out and subsequently seduce as high a number of fine females as possible, whilst also eliminating any need to walk around in order to meet people. He preferred to just sit, drink, and see what happened; especially on nights such as this one, when his right leg had been troubling him more than usual.

    No sooner had he sat down, than Beni appeared. Her eyes lit up as soon as she saw Clarke – as was always the case – and she immediately came over, almost *strutting* as she made her way to greet him. Beni looked especially good tonight. She wore a black skirt that was short, but not so short as to take away the mystery. The thing with Ms. Rothwell was that she always endeavoured to leave something to the imagination, both in how she dressed *and* talked. She'd opted for a tight fitting red top, which matched the flecks of auburn in her hair. Her make-up was exemplary, as always; not overdone, but just enough to add a subtle touch of sassiness. Male heads turned as she strode over to Rossiter's side of the bar, such was the glamorous air that Beni exuded. She knew this only too well. She was aware that she had an aura, something that always made men stop and look. She could have been an actress, playing to the camera as she did, although it was always very much tongue in cheek. A typically beaming smile greeted Clarke as she came to serve the Playhouse's most famous customer.

  "Mr. Rossiter! How are you? I presume work today wasn't too hard on academia's favourite son, given that you're still here tonight to tell the tale! And thirsty too! Am I right?"

  "Dead right, Beni! Got most of my preparation done for when the real fun starts in a few days!"

"What'll it be? Bourbon?"

"No. Gimme a beer to start with. Never a good idea to begin proceedings by hittin' the hard stuff too early!"

"Right you are, Clarkey boy! Just gimme a minute…"

As Beni went off in search of Rossiter's liquid refreshment, he scanned the bar, looking left and right. The Playhouse was quiet, given that it was still relatively early. He hoped that things would liven up a little later, as was usually the case. At the moment there were only a handful of women in the whole place, and of the sparse smattering, only one who was even *close* to being acceptable. *Good looking* would have been pushing it, however.

Rossiter was interrupted in his reverie by Beni sliding his beer along the bar, followed by a thumbs up and her trademark smile. It was warm, friendly and endearing, but cheeky and slightly mischievous at the same time.

Beni and Clarke had become close friends over the years. They had a relaxed, drama free relationship, devoid of any complications, which suited them both. It surprised Rossiter somewhat that things had never progressed beyond friendship. But this was probably because neither of them had ever hinted at or pushed for anything more, which was probably a good thing. If Congletown's lovable lothario had learnt anything, it was that once feelings usurped fellatio, and sentiment superseded sex, drama was never far away. Feelings were usually something talked about by women, not men. An arbitrary notion, a blanket term applied to people interested in other people, but who weren't quite sure how to articulate said interest. Thus, these often emotionally vulnerable people announced their feelings to the object of their desires. Feelings of what, exactly, Rossiter had never been entirely sure. Why use such an abstract term if you didn't know exactly what it meant? Especially given that the proclamation of these "feelings" almost *never* led to anywhere good. Clarke wasn't against expressing himself, but there was a time and place for everything. Emotionally unburdening oneself to the object of one´s innermost desires was irresponsible, reckless, rash, and potentially damaging to both parties. As such, Rossiter had long since ordained that even if the day should ever come (and it hadn't yet) where he may begin to feel anything more than a desire for simple interaction - and intercourse - with a woman, he would be sure to tread very carefully. In the vast majority of cases, once a guy chose to tell a girl how he felt, it was curtains, game over, *goodnight, Vienna…*

    Rossiter took one final swig of his beer, before immediately ordering number two. As he sipped, three or four fellow drinkers acknowledged him with a nod and a wave as they walked by, such was his fame and notoriety in this place. The Playhouse was home to a number of intriguing characters. But Clarke was the one everyone really wanted to be. Sure, he loved women. But he was also very respectful towards them, and guys he met too, assuming that they behaved in the same way towards him. Whilst it was true that Rossiter didn't like everyone, and certain individuals annoyed, aggravated or bored him on occasion, he always attempted to behave respectfully and with class towards everyone with whom he interacted. His parents, especially his mother, had brought him up well, teaching him to be polite and well mannered. Rossiter wasn't perfect, far from it. But he lived his life the way *he* wanted to, and respected everybody else into the bargain. He had always held strong values of integrity, honesty and respect – those passed on to him by his parents – and he believed that these values were the sign of a true man. He had his faults, and numerous they were. But Rossiter had always been extremely self - confident, without being arrogant. He had never *needed* to be, and he saw arrogance as one of the most unattractive traits, as would any lady worthy of the name. There was a time for being serious and working hard. But the majority of the time, Clarke's outlook on life was that it were to be enjoyed. Not a *game* per se – although the professor *was* a formidable player when in the mood – but something fun, and not to be taken *too* seriously! He was here for a good time, not a long time, and he always attempted to make the best use of said time. So what better place to start than The Playhouse on a Friday night.

  He glanced almost disinterestedly to his right. A reasonably attractive girl sidled up to the bar and stood next to him, before ordering a drink. She was cute – most men would probably even say *very* cute – but to Rossiter, she was nothing more than another one in a long line of what he referred to as *copy and paste cuties*. Her beverage arrived, a Mojito - how very unoriginal! She flashed a feeble smile Clarke's way and sat down next to him, sipping on her minty refreshment. As she looked across at him again, Rossiter couldn't help but allow a smirk to escape from his lips. He could tell straight away that she was one of those attention - seeking, Instagram obsessed party girls. Her second smile was bordering on a pout, and it smacked of the deserving diva type of arrogance that was becoming increasingly common in young women these days. All boobs and no brain cells. Not only the way this particular girl looked, but her whole demeanour, was fake. So many women from around the age of twenty – three to twenty – eight these days gave the impression that they believed any man should count himself lucky to even be in their company. These incessant party – goers smacked of self – importance, were usually devoid of intelligence, and completely lacking in any social awareness. Such creatures preyed upon men who they saw as a soft touch. A way to pass the time, inflate their already huge egos, and use the enticing entrapment of legs, lips and lashes to procure free drinks from the latest sucker who decided to put them on a pedestal, or simply lacked the balls to say no to their self – entitled advances.

    Rossiter was all for treating the ladies well; that should be a given for *any* man. But it was the attention seekers who craved the limelight and believed they automatically deserved free drinks from guys just because they looked even half way cute, and had made the dubious effort to don a dress – often one that showed more ass than class – that both irritated and amused him. The recent wave of new age feminism had allowed today's social media generation to believe that they automatically deserved attention and respect from their male counterparts merely because they were women, regardless of the fact that much of the behaviour flagrantly exhibited by the majority of them lacked any traits with even a semblance of femininity. It seemed to Clarke that although the majority of young women today demanded respect, they very rarely showed any to men on the receiving end, and this irked him somewhat.

However, given that he was nearing the end of his latest drink, and the night was thus far proving somewhat tedious, he decided to play along, just for fun:

"Hi there. I'm Clarke."

"I'm very happy for you…"

"What might *your* name be?"

"Get me another drink, and I might think about tellin' you…" she replied with another forced smile that bordered on a superior, self – congratulatory sneer.

"Would that be a Mojito? With all those mouthfuls of minty majesty?"

"Huh…? Uh… yeah, it's a Mojito."

"I'm not sure I can, I'm afraid. I never trust cocktail drinking women. They make me lose my Mo-jo… Okay, that wasn't my finest play on words, I'll grant you! It needs work. My opening lines aren't quite what they used to be, and I'm not even sure that you understood what I just said, anyway!

But I'm gonna need to know more about you before I agree to buy you another beverage with a view to prolonging this conversation, loaded though it may be with potential…"

She looked back at him bemusedly, not quite sure how to react or respond. She'd sat down next to the best looking man at the bar, in the hope of getting a drink. It wasn't too hard to understand, surely! But this guy spoke to her in a language which may as well have been Chinese! What was his deal?

"What's your name?"

"Mandy"

"Great to meet you, Mandy! What brings you to our little corner of paradise?"

"What?"

"Why… are… you … here…?"

"Oh. I just wanted a drink, and to see if there were any cute guys here tonight…" she replied with a self – important flick of the hair.

"I see! And… have you found any?"

The puckering pout returned; "Well… *you're* not too bad I suppose. For an old guy. Get me another of these and maybe we'll talk some more…" She subsequently reached into her designer bag and took out her phone, before positioning the cocktail in prime selfie position and snapping away, complete with yet another perfect pout, doubtless for Insta's benefit. Oh, her parents must be so *very* proud, Rossiter thought to himself.

"Okay, so... Tell me the most exciting thing you did today, Mandy? And also something interesting about yourself? Maybe *then* we'll see about that drink…"

She almost glared back at her by now slightly inebriated interlocutor, seemingly incredulous at having been questioned as to whether or not she *deserved* a drink! Being made to jump through men's hoops was apparently an alien concept to today's twenty - something, fame – seeking, female fornicators…

"Uh, well… I went to the gym. But only for two hours today. My friend and I had a date at a day spa later, so I had to cut short my workout. Again.

Hey… does my ass look fat?"

"Negative. And something interesting?"

Deep in thought, with a puzzled expression now etched upon her face, she seemed at a loss for something to say. However, the look of confusion subsequently disappeared almost as quickly as it had arrived, as her face suddenly lit up as she thought of something to hopefully wow the old man with! It was almost a eureka moment… or you – reek – ahhh… such was the excessive amount of cheap perfume unleashed upon that most scowling of faces. A marriage of fragrance and foundation, Mojito and make – up which was likely to make the majority of this town's fine gentlemen run for the hills…

"I got it! I did a social media photo shoot, and our football team's star player's brother's girlfriend was in the background! Everyone knows her, and she has the *best* hair! Oh my God, it was *amazing*! Hihihihi!"

Rossiter looked back at her, smiled almost apologetically, finished his drink, and stood up to leave.

"Hey, Mister! Where's my drink?! You promised!"

"Oh, I'm sorry Mandy, but Mojitos wait for no man, and I've got somewhere to be. It's not far from here, but the journey may potentially be hazardous. Enjoy your night… and be sure to look out for any more rogue footballing imposters attempting to steal your social media thunder online!"

"Asshole! You fucking promised!"

Rossiter made his way around to the other side of the bar, affording himself a smirk upon seeing Mojito Mandy storm angrily out of the Playhouse, slamming the door as she left. He hadn't intended to be mean to her, but he had met so many girls like her over the years, that he just didn't have the time, energy or desire to be in their company any longer. The bar continued to fill up, but it wasn't exceedingly busy just yet. It was approaching eleven thirty. Given that more customers had arrived, there were now relatively few empty seats and quiet places left at the bar. Clarke eventually found a rare bit of vacant space, along with an unoccupied stool. He sat down and ordered another beer. He had decided that this one would be his last, and that he would then move onto the hard stuff – probably bourbon.

When his latest beverage arrived, he took a sip, once again contemplating the familiar surroundings. The beer was good, but he felt unusually tired, probably as a consequence of that morning's work, along with the mental fatigue caused by the monotonous and mundane preparation and administrative paperwork that academia seemed so bewilderingly fond of. Clarke enjoyed his job most of the time, and although he didn't belong to that group of academics who had an incredible passion for their work – he found them utterly pretentious – he acknowledged that being in a position to be able to educate people and watch them develop and improve, had its merits. In short, his job wasn't too bad, most of the time. It kept him busy, paid the bills, and went at least some way to preventing him from drinking even *more* than he already did. Rossiter had always been an uncomplicated man. Right from his early days as a university student, where he had studied French and English Lit *and* clit, he had always known what life was about for him: literature, liquor and ladies.

He finished his beer and surprised himself somewhat by deciding not to order another drink. His leg was still troubling him, and he saw no reason to stay at the bar when he wasn't really feeling in the mood. There were a few late evening drinkers still arriving, but no girls that he had even the slightest interest in attempting to entertain. He motioned Beni over, settled his tab, and subsequently reached for his jacket off the back of another nearby chair, turning his head to collect his change in the process. He pulled again at his jacket in an attempt to prise it from the back of the chair, and began to get impatient when it surprisingly refused to budge. Growing increasingly annoyed, Rossiter felt a hand on his right shoulder which startled him somewhat, and turned agitatedly around:

"Mr. Rossiter! Leaving so soon…?"

The voice was soft and playful, but also direct and unwavering in posing the question. Clarke spun on his barstool, all of the previous discomfort in his lower limbs vanishing in a flash as he turned to face his interlocutor. Even before he swivelled to look, he knew exactly who had asked the question.

She was back.

There she was, standing just a few inches in front of him, right hand on the back of his chair - hence his bemused sense of failure in having attempted to wrestle away his jacket mere seconds earlier – and that most petite of left hands lodged on her shapely hip in a stance that both demanded attention and screamed seduction.

The Frenchy…

Rossiter was accustomed to regular contact with a multitude of magnificent Mädchens. And although he revelled in his regular trips to the Playhouse in order to think, drink and *sink the pink* with a whole host of feisty Fräuleins, they were merely a means to an end, a distraction, an enjoyable way of passing the time with somebody, *anybody*, as opposed to seeking solace in companionship of the liquid variety. Clarke had long since grasped the concept of a beer or bourbon being like an old, trusted friend in many ways; you knew what you were getting, and they'd never let you down, but the outcome was always the same.

While friends equated to beer and the proverbial safe ground, women were like cocktails. Meeting and seducing a new woman was, for Rossiter, comparable to taking that first taste of a new, exotic drink; the tongue delving into unchartered territory to take a sip and be seduced by that intoxicating liquor, that ravishing recipe known – to us mere mortals - as *woman*. You never knew exactly what you were getting with a new woman. And that, for Clarke, was why they were so much fun.

Women were one of life's great mysteries and pleasures for Rossiter. But of all the women he had met, there had only ever been one who had provoked anything more than mild amusement or intrigue, and stayed on his mind. It had been a while since they'd first met. He'd indulged in liaisons with various girls throughout that time, so it wasn't as though he'd been 'hung up' on the Frenchy, or anyone else for that matter.
But she had intrigued him more than any of the others, and he'd subsequently thought of her occasionally.
And now here she was.

As soon as the question had left her lips, he'd known immediately who had asked it. That voice was unmistakable; he understood instinctively to whom the enquiring mouth belonged. He took a moment to compose himself, before adjusting his position and turning around to face this most welcome and unexpected of drinking companions.

Nothing, however, could have prepared him for what came next. Having turned around, he looked up at her, and all his hastily gathered composure vanished in a heartbeat. Indeed, Rossiter's heart was beating so fast and so hard that he almost feared it (not to mention *another* vital organ) would burst out from within. Clarke was no stranger to rhythmic pounding, but of a totally different nature, and the vision before him was a sight to behold.

She had maintained exactly the same pose; right hand atop the chair, left hand still on hip, almost caressing the tight fitting, figure – hugging fabric of a dauntingly delicious, deep red dress, the likes of which Rossiter had never seen. It – and *she* – dazzled him.

"Miss Lejeune! Always a pleasure! What brings you back to these parts? It's been a while…"

The soft, seductive smile returned to those most luscious, almost lascivious of lips, as she slowly edged around the vacant barstool and sat down to Rossiter's right. He noticed that she took extra care not to fall, and having ensured that she be sitting as comfortably as possible, looked directly at Clarke, those blue – green emerald eyes still sparkling just as they had on their first meeting. Her eye contact was powerful yet playful, and Rossiter assumed that she probably used it to enrapture, enthrall and ensnare men on a regular basis, as did he when in pursuit of women. It was a game he knew well and was always eager to play, especially with Analisse Lejeune, who had so surprisingly reappeared in his life.

"I had a tough day and haven't been out around here for a while, so thought I'd stop by for a drink."

"Say no more! What'll it be? Malibu, if memory serves?"

"I'm impressed, Mr Rossiter. You remembered!"

"Some things are hard to forget…"

"Well, chapeau, as we say back home! Top marks for Clarke!"

"Beni! A bourbon for me, and a Malibu and pineapple juice for my favourite French fancy, if you please!"

The bartender acknowledged her favourite customer's order with a wry, knowing smile bordering on a smirk.

"No problem, Clarke. Coming up!"

As she walked away to get their drinks, Analisse – or Ana, as her friends apparently called her – shuffled towards Clarke so that their conversation could continue:

"So, Mr. Rossiter… actually, let's just go with Clarke, it's so much less formal… I have three questions."

"Hit me."

"Okay. Let's get the (potentially) boring stuff out of the way first. What's new in the world of Mister Clarke Rossiter?"

Her smile often seemed cheeky in a way Clarke couldn't quite put his finger on, especially when she asked questions. It almost appeared as though she were quizzing him, with just the slightest hint of self –

satisfaction creeping across her face as a knowing smile escaped from her lips.

Rossiter raised his glass in Ana's direction, as if to signal his satisfaction at being in her company once again after a considerable hiatus. With a contented smile, he took a sip of bourbon, the legendary lothario's favourite larynx lubricator, before continuing:

"Well, sorry to disappoint, but the events of the past week have been somewhat mundane, Miss Lejeune. Mainly just work. That's not to say that I don't like my profession, or parts of it. But it rarely changes from day to day, with the exception of an occasional unforeseen dilemma or an irritating colleague, my vocation is more monotonous than magical. But enough of my working woes! I never talk about my professional life, for the very simple reason that I don't like to or *want* to. So, I'm not going to start this evening. Next question?"

Analisse took a sip of her drink, still looking straight at Rossiter as she did so. She'd been surprised and maybe even a little frustrated at his refusal to discuss his work. Clarke's employment wasn't particularly significant to her, at least not in these very early stages of their getting to know one another. She merely wanted to find out as much as possible about him; the fact that he didn't appear to be quite the open book that she'd hoped for simply meant that she would have to work a bit harder to wipe the dust from that battle – hardened cover and pry it open, before embarking upon the first page of what promised to be quite the intriguing tale. Or so she hoped...

Ana had always considered herself a better reader of people than of books. Her first impressions and general assessments of the individuals she met were usually fairly accurate; her only shortcoming was a tendency to be too nice to people on occasion, letting them get away with too much and thus taking advantage of her good nature. It could be said that this naivety was sometimes her undoing, although recent experiences had served as helpful lessons in the putting up of barriers to avoid being hurt, as she had so often been in the past. With regard to the written word, Analisse had always been a conscientious student, but she only ever read what was deemed *essential* by teachers, and seldom delved into the depths of the literary canon as a means of pleasure or entertainment. Rossiter, however, appeared to be articulate and interesting. His turn of phrase and seemingly extensive vocabulary, coupled with the fact that he was handsome in his own way, made him all the more intriguing. Ana had never attached much importance to whether a man be particularly good looking or not. As far as she was concerned, one's physical attributes were insignificant in and of themselves, merely a potential bonus. What really intrigued and attracted her was a man's intelligence. Tonight's second meeting with Clarke had confirmed her interest in him. He amused her and heightened her curiosity, but she didn't get the impression that this was forced, pretentious or disingenuous in any way. Although she barely knew Rossiter, her initial reading of him was positive. He seemed fun to be around, and he also made her feel significant, safe and secure. It was by virtue of these qualities, and in the hope of discovering yet more, that she wanted to get to *faire plus ample connaissance.*

    Rossiter remained perched on his barstool mere feet away, sipping contemplatively on his drink, eyes fixed intently on Ana. A wry, playful smile now graced his lips, which glistened once again following the latest intake of bourbon. Ana got the impression that Clarke was now more relaxed. Any nerves or surprise that she had sensed in him earlier – albeit only for a matter of seconds after she had re-introduced herself – now appeared to have vanished and, as he continued sipping and looking directly back at her, she sensed that the glint which she had been so attracted to and captivated by upon their first meeting all those weeks ago had returned to his eye. She looked back at him with a smile that mirrored his own, and continued with her questioning:

"Question number two, Mr. Rossiter: Have you got alcohol back at your place?"

Clarke smirked, not deeming an answer necessary, such was the absurdity of the question. He acquiesced wordlessly, prompting Ana to ask her third and final one:

"How much might a taxi be at this time of night?" she enquired, taking one final sip of Malibu before placing her empty glass on the bar, winking at him in a way that was both delicate and deadly in equal measure, and putting into words what they'd both been thinking since they'd crossed paths again:

"Let's get out of here…"

4.

Nothing more needed to be said. Not another word left either of their lips as they left the Playhouse, although they both smiled as the recently reacquainted left the bar, having grabbed their jackets, and Clarke his cane.

As Analisse got off her barstool and shuffled around to join him, Rossiter noticed something somewhat unusual in her gait. He cast his mind back to the night they had first met, and remembered having noticed a slight limp as his new companion had gone off in search of the bathroom. He hadn't thought much of it at the time. Maybe she'd had an accident, or some minor everyday injury that had "put her on the back foot", so to speak. Or perhaps it was something more serious. But in any case, it didn't matter. She was a more than welcome new arrival. The latest on his conveyor belt of *cracking crumpet*.

However, despite his being accustomed to beautiful women and comfortable in their presence, Clarke had always had the feeling – ever since that first night, and even now – that Ana was different. Aside from the fact that her beauty was unparalleled in the purely physical sense; the hair, the dancing eyes, and oh Lord, tonight's almost *demonic* dress which clung to her, enveloped her, almost seeming to hold all of that fantasy – inducing feminine flesh hostage, bathing in a sexy sea of red, Rossiter was *intrigued* by her. He'd known that since their first meeting. But while

women and intrigue were nothing new to him, Analisse Lejeune was. Or she at least had the *potential* to be. So as they left the bar together, with Rossiter's right hand on his cane, and the other playfully caressing Ana's fabulous French fingers, Clarke sensed that he was edging ever closer to the proverbial promised land. In holding her hand, he also held the keys to the kingdom. But for Analisse Lejeune - the new French femme fatale – to grant him access and unlock the door to a world of inner treasures and carnal pleasures, Rossiter needed to pull out all the stops.
As they stood outside on the pavement, hailed a taxi and subsequently arrived home, he knew he was ready...

5.

Rossiter paid the fare and they both shuffled out of the cab. In spite of his cane, Clarke attempted not just to walk up the path to his front door, but to *stride*, in a manner of speaking. He always tried to show confidence in both his words and his actions, and he believed that a strong gait would aid him in exuding the self - assurance that he deemed so important not merely in the seducing of women, but life in general. He smirked, however, with the subsequent realisation that tonight's mixture of beer and bourbon had put paid to any hopes of walking confidently. As he tottered towards the door, still holding Ana's hand, he sensed that tonight was going to be interesting...

He rummaged in his pocket for the front door key, unlocked, and let

Ana past him into the hall. Ladies first, and all that. Rossiter was nothing if not chivalrous. He took Ana's jacket from her before removing his own and hanging them both up. And the red dress was there again, in all its splendour! He *genuinely* had never seen a garment quite like it. It teased him, tempted him, in much the same way as its wearer. But while Ana had what might have been described as a subtle sassiness about her, the dress just *screamed* sexuality. It was beautiful yet brash, bold, blatant. And he loved it.

He walked into the kitchen to assess the liquid refreshment options. The cupboard was well stocked with an impressive range of wines, and a vast array of other beverages to suit even the most discerning of drinkers. Clarke smirked once again as he noticed a bottle of Malibu, slender and white, flanked by one of Rossiter's favourite single malts, and on the other side, an as yet unopened bottle of Cognac. The assembly of various bottles in the cupboard were not ordered in any particular way. Clarke always just put them back in there any old how, and had no rules as to what should go where in his alcove of alcoholic ammunition. It was merely by chance that the Malibu found itself with whiskey on one side and Cognac on the other; almost like two reputable gentlemen standing watch over a lady in white, keeping her safe and secure. The tapping of Analisse's dainty red high heels on the kitchen floor startled him somewhat, and reminded him that he needed to get his head back in the game.

"What'll it be, Ana? I have quite the selection of alcoholic beverages here... even Malibu, would you believe?! I presume that will once again be your weapon of choice?"

Her response surprised him:

"You presume wrongly, Señor Rossiter! I'd be intrigued to see what *else* you may be able to tempt me with..."

Ana winked as she answered, once again showing that playfulness which made her all the more attractive not only to Clarke, but doubtless to any man ever to have the pleasure of her company.

Without further ado, Rossiter withdrew a bottle of Australian Shiraz from the cupboard. She may well be French, but Clarke had never understood all the chauvinistic hype surrounding French wine, or *anything* French for that matter. It was unwise to generalise. But having spent time in France, Rossiter had always been irked – but also smirked – at the pretentious arrogance of so many Frenchies with regard to their food, drink, and customs. They were perfectly entitled (and right) to be proud of their produce and traditions. But it had often seemed to him that the vast majority of them held the view that if something wasn't French, it couldn't possibly be any good. The French seemingly loved to not only laud their own things, but also to look down upon anything from anywhere else. It was the attitude of *si ce n'est pas français, ce n'est pas bon* that had always irritated Clarke. Analisse was quite marvellous, however, and he had almost chosen a rare bottle of Merlot for her to try, before deciding against it. Tonight she would be drinking Aussie!

"I have it on very good authority that this Australian red is delightful! None of this French rubbish!"

He smirked as he opened said Shiraz, pouring two generous glasses, handing Ana hers before taking his own. They clinked, both smiling, although hers was more one of shock and defiance than amusement, and they each took a sip.

"Verdict on the vino, Miss Lejeune ?"

She took another sip, making the most glorious lip smacking sound, before answering, with a satisfied smile:

"Not bad, Mr. Rossiter. Not bad at all. In fact it's so good, it could *almost* be French..." she said with yet another playful wink.

"Right. And we could *almost* be professional athletes. But I'm often more paraletic than Paralympic. And as for throwing the hammer? Well, I just prefer *getting* hammered..."

"Ah, very drole, Clarkey boy, very drole. And so early in the proceedings, too. But be warned: any mention of your (spam) javelin, and I'm out of here!"

"Haha! Why, Miss Lejeune... you're quite funny too... for a Frenchy..." With that, Rossiter motioned his guest into the living room with a nonchalant hand gesture. He took her glass from her and she sat down on the couch, before accepting her wine back from him. Clarke launched his cane onto the floor, and duly took his place next to her.

"So tell me, Ana. What's the story? I mean, I know alarmingly little about you, save for an occasional flick of the hair, dazzling eyes, and a dress that could wake the dead! I'm going to call you Ana, rather than Analisse, if it's all the same with you. I mean, I'm generally a smooth talker. But with your name being so exotic, I struggle to get my tongue around the 'lisse' part. Which may be surprising to you, as French oral is often said to be one of my strong points. Quite the cunning linguist, if you will..."

Rossiter's latest attempt at a *jeu de mots,* however crass, nevertheless amused Ana, although she was also slightly guarded and unsure of herself. She afforded herself a nervous laugh, before turning back to face Clarke and taking another sip of wine. Although not from her homeland, it *was* good. She had to give the man his due; he certainly appeared to know his Merlot from his Malbec.

"I have a suggestion for you, Mr. Rossiter. Entertaining though your turn of phrase may be, how about cooling it with the remarks which ladies with not so thick a skin as mine would probably deem borderline offensive, and telling me more about yourself. You've just said that you know very little about me. Well, I might say the same of you. You clearly have a way with words, so why not use said gift more positively and actually try *talking* to me, rather than hiding behind a whirlwind of witticisms and hurricane of hyperbole? As fascinating as you (probably) are, I get the impression you're still more bard than bawdy. So stop trying so hard, and let's just get to know one another better. Do we have a deal?"

"That we do, Miss Lejeune. Let's drink to that!"

Rossiter stood up from the armchair he'd previously been sitting in, and walked over to join Analisse on the couch, raising his glass with a smile as he did so.

"To conversation!" She nodded and they clinked glasses again.

"So, Ana, this whole *deep and meaningful* conversation stuff is pretty new territory for me. Unchartered waters, if you will. As such, I'd like to start the ball rolling with the first obvious question that comes to mind. I've noticed on numerous occasions that your way of walking is a little out of the ordinary. Rather like my own, in fact, minus the cane. Care to enlighten me?"

The directness of Rossiter's opening question, and so early in the proceedings, appeared to unnerve Ana somewhat. The ensuing sip of wine from her glass, which was now half empty, appeared to get lodged in her throat before a slight cough duly sent it on its way. She hoped a refill would be imminent.

"Little's Syndrome. Next question?"

Her riposte was as unsettling as *she* was unsettled. It was quick, with Ana looking away from her interlocutor almost as though she wanted not merely to gloss over the question, but to dismiss it entirely. Agitated. Nervous. Resentful at having been asked. Ana's reaction both surprised and intrigued Rossiter. He had always been comfortable with his own disability and its inherent limitations, or at least the limitations that others undoubtedly perceived him to have. The abrupt nature of Analisse's answer appeared to indicate that this was not the case for her. She immediately seemed reluctant to acknowledge her own physical shortcomings, or at least to discuss them. He could identify with that, even though his own outlook differed slightly. It drew her closer to him in an instant.

He focused on her, his brown eyes using the silence to search for a sign, contemplating her with a view to finding out more, an attempt to unearth something else that, as yet, he was not quite sure of. Analisse managed to muster a flustered, almost apologetic smile before returning to her glass, either as a way of escaping Clarke's questions, or as a means of inviting him to continue with the interrogation, if he so chose.

"Come on, don't be shy. I didn't mean to unsettle you. It just seemed like a pretty obvious place to start. I'm always curious whenever I meet a new woman, and I suppose I hoped the fact that we both have a disability would give us ammunition as a conversation starter. Congratulations! You have succeeded in intriguing me more than most of the mademoiselles that pass through these hallowed halls! So come on, we can regale each other in discussing our various ailments. Elephant in the room... be gone with you!"

Ana really didn't know how to react. Although it was usually extremely difficult to suppress a smile when in Clarke's company, such was his power of seduction, clever sense of humour and a mastery of language that she had never encountered in anyone else, her spiky reaction to these latest questions was perhaps testament to the fact that she was beginning to feel mildly *irritated* by him. How could he be so *comfortable* in that beautiful skin of his? So accepting of his disability and confident in who he was? She wasn't entirely sure whether she envied or admired him. Perhaps it was actually a mixture of both that irked her. She'd never been a confident person herself, either socially or academically. She easily got stressed and flustered at things which really weren't that important. She recalled one occasion a couple of years earlier, when she'd been preparing with a friend for an oral presentation at school. The person in question had helped her, she had all of her notes, and was ready to go. Or so she thought. But before a word had even left her mouth, the heavy breathing and shaking had started, culminating in a bout of stress that had bordered on a panic attack. And all of that for a presentation being practised at *home*, and with somebody she knew well. So it would be fair to say that she was a "worrier" who often struggled to deal with stressful situations. It was sometimes almost as though she went out of her way either to exacerbate problems, or to create ones that weren't even there.

She'd often wondered whether there was a direct link between her propensity to stress, and the fact that her disability made her so uncomfortable. Analisse, consciously or otherwise, had always done everything in her power to deflect attention away from the fact that her legs, beautiful though she knew they were – as numerous men had told her so – didn't quite work in the way that they should. Was she just a stressed out person anyway? Or was it conceivable that her anguish at what she perceived as her physical limitations also manifested itself in her staggering lack of confidence in other situations; in social or academic circles, for example? Thus, Ana had done her utmost to ignore her disability. She never drew attention to it, only discussing it when pressed, and never through choice. Even her photos endeavoured to hide the fact that through no fault of her own, she wasn't the perfect embodiment of flawless femininity that she believed society judged to be the benchmark for all women her age nowadays. Analisse Lejeune wasn't perfect, and believed that her disability served to accentuate those imperfections. She was almost in denial about it, but it was easier than acceptance. The fact that unlike her, the man sitting just a few inches away seemed to be so accepting, confident and in control of himself and his own reality, was almost certainly the reason for Ana's annoyance at Clarke's latest questions. He himself had guessed that this were the case, and her response was therefore not surprising.

"Sorry if I was a bit abrupt there. I prefer not to talk about my disability if I can help it. "Disability" is such an ugly word, after all. As though we need some kind of label to highlight the fact that we can't do certain things. Whether the likes of you and I would even *want* to do them, almost seems secondary! Or maybe I'm just another wannabe academic getting bogged down in semantics in spite of herself..."

"Well.... I believe that we're on the same page. *Les intellectuels à deux francs m'ennuient*, as somebody highly esteemed once said. The likes of you and I do not need labels. We are what we are, our legs will hereby remain nameless works of art, to be revered rather than sneered at! And in case you've forgotten, with you in that most delectable of dresses, and me on my cane, you and I will always be the real stars of the show! Our very own *Festival de Can(n)es...*"

"Haha! Oh blooooody hell! That was *good*! You're on fire tonight, Mister!"

"Why, thank you!"

Analisse edged closer to Clarke, and they once again touched glasses. She looked back at him, smiling, with any previous sense of uneasiness having been vanquished. He took another sip, and placed his right hand on her thigh, running his fingers along it, from bottom to top. He looked at her, and he could tell that she *wanted* him. There was a longing in her eyes, almost an aching. He could both see and feel how turned on she was getting. He leaned in towards her, his right hand having moved from her leg, and now caressing her shoulders and sliding down her back, with his as yet unoccupied left hand reaching around the back of Ana's neck, before sliding her smooth brown hair back and whispering into her ear:

"Are you ready for me...?"

Rossiter looked her in the eye as he said this. A deep, penetrating look harbouring honesty, steely determination, and just a hint of vulnerability. Not to be confused with weakness. They weren't – and aren't – the same thing.

With his eyes fixed on her, he moved and planted a soft, lingering kiss on her naked, unprotected neck. It was little more than a peck; a mere brushing of lip upon neckline that caused Analisse to gasp, arching her back in acknowledgement of both the eroticism of the situation, and in anticipation of what was hopefully to come. Rossiter took her right hand, picked her up off the couch, and led her to the bedroom...

6.

As Clarke kicked open the bedroom door with his right foot, struggling to master the movement of his cane in the process, Ana whispered to him:

"I don't *normally* do this! Not on the first night..."

"It's not the first night, we've already met, remember. Don't worry, baby!" He put her down on the bed. A mirage of white sheets and red dress that seemed both erotic and repulsive at once. Clarke had always *hated* red and white as a combination. But that dress. Oh, God. He could make an exception.

As Ana fell back onto the bed, Clarke made sure that she was comfortable, then placed a hand on each of her shoulders and proceeded to unzip the red dress. As he placed his right thumb and forefinger upon the opening, brass zipper gliding effortlessly against edges that yielded easily, offering little resistance, it appeared almost to be a ritual of sorts. The ravishing redness duly slid away, and he was in.

What lay underneath was even more spectacular than Rossiter had ever dared to imagine. He had always adored red underwear on a woman. He wasn't entirely sure why. Probably because it symbolised everything he found enchanting about the fairer sex; eroticism, lust, danger.

There she was, Analisse Lejeune, all in red. Under that almost mythical of dresses, there she lay in bra and knickers. She looked a little bit tentative. Not nervous, *per se*, but almost as though she wasn't quite sure what to expect. As though she needed guidance. He sat her up, and kissed her neck again, as he'd done only a few moments previously. As he attempted to massage her shoulders – a skill many a beautiful woman had previously told him he was a dab hand at – he sensed that Ana was tense. He drew her brown hair back, those beautiful, glorious locks, and whispered softly into her ear:

"Don't worry. We'll only do what we're *both* comfortable with. Ok?"
She acquiesced with a groan.
Taking Ana's satisfied moanings as the green light to continue, Rossiter turned her around to look at her once more. She was beautiful. No, more

than that; Analisse Lejeune was absolutely *spectacular*!

Rossiter had often thought about and compared the merits of various types of ladies' underwear. He was able to appreciate the female undergarment in all of its glorious forms. Provided, of course, that the lady sporting them was worthy of their grandeur. In his years of philandering, Clarke had seen countless female *fesses*, a veritable bonanza of beautiful backsides. But he had long since drawn the conclusion that as gloriously tempting, seductive and sexy as a woman's body often was, the beauty of the female form and all of its incumbent delights was very often accentuated and rendered all the more beautiful, by virtue of the garments chosen to enrobe it.

He turned Ana around, so that her back was to him. Rossiter went to her neck again, left a light, lingering touch of the lips on the right side, subsequently tracing the forefinger of each hand downwards, before starting to massage her shoulders, whispering into her ear once again:

"You're tense. Relax, Ana. If there's anything you don't like, or if something doesn't feel good, or whatever, just let me know. Ok?"

"Ok" she whispered, barely audibly.

She looked phenomenal, but as delicious as the sight before him was, a veritable red velvet vixen, Rossiter was getting increasingly turned on, and he sensed Ana was too. He wanted to unearth his treasure:

"I'm going to unwrap you like a Christmas present. I'm going to touch, kiss, caress every centimetre... no... every millimetre... of you..."

Analisse´s whimpering gradually turned into moaning, as Clarke once again moved down her neck and across her shoulders, before venturing south and unhooking Ana's bra. The sound as the clasp gave way was one of surrender. Music to Rossiter's ears. He was the master of symphonies in this tantalisingly melodic orchestra! Now all that remained was for him to unleash his instrument and proceed.

As her bra fell down onto the bed, Ana unexpectedly turned to face Clarke. She appeared to be enjoying the mounting sexual tension, but still appeared slightly unsure of exactly what to expect.

It was almost unheard of for Analisse Lejeune to give up her body as she was doing tonight, and especially to a relative stranger. She just wasn't that kind of girl. Or at least, not normally.

Rossiter had learned long ago that men and women were totally different with regard to sex and sexuality. Of course, the purely physical aspect of any relationship – especially of a sexual nature – was important to both fellas *and* females. But at the end of the day, regardless of gender, we're all mere mammals; carnal, animalistic, sometimes even brutal upon occasion. But the majority of the male population are enticed, excited and stimulated *visually*. As men, we're generally far more turned on by a pert pair of breasts, sexy legs, or a delicious derrière. For the ladies, however, while physical appearance undoubtedly plays a part, they are more likely to be drawn to potential suitors as a consequence of words spoken, or a gesture, an act, a *feeling*. Rossiter understood – unlike the vast majority of men his age, or indeed any other age – that women's attraction stimuli were almost never physical, but *emotional*. Acknowledging this, Clarke took both of Ana's hands - petite, feminine, almost feline - and turned her around to face him again:

"Ana, you are absolutely sensational. Not just tonight; I knew it from the very first moment I ever laid eyes on you..."

Reassured, and becoming increasingly turned on, she leaned in towards Clarke, attempting to kiss him for the very first time. But he withdrew, deliberately and without hesitation. Ana's female psychology cogs began whirring relentlessly again: *doesn't he like me? Is he just playing games like men do? Why is he pulling away*?

Women do that. They have an alarming tendency to over analyse everything, looking for a solution to any number of non-existent problems. Ana's female psyche was attempting to do just that. It was etched all over her face, and also demonstrated in her body language. Rossiter's apparent refusal – or at least reluctance – to kiss her had caused her to doubt herself, as she was often prone to doing. Ana moved away from her conqueror, endeavouring to cover her newly disrobed body in an apparent showing of modesty. She'd wanted to kiss him and he'd apparently rejected her. Ana regrettably believed she had no choice but to pull away from the professor, albeit only a matter of inches. But she needn't have worried:
Having released Analisse's hands from his grasp, Rossiter looked directly at her, maintaining his revered steely, unwavering eye contact as a means of showing her that he was in control. Powerful and dominant, without being threatening:

"Listen, Ana. This is very important. I *do* want to kiss you, and I'm going to, but not yet. I said to you before, that I want to explore you, enjoy you, savour you. However, to do that, we both need to take our time, and not rush things. I could tell that you backed away when I didn't kiss you before. And now I'm going to explain to you *why* I showed such restraint..."

He moved towards her again and took hold of her, almost cradling her in his arms, as though he were protecting her, safeguarding her, shielding her both from himself and from the outside world.

Analisse stared back at him, in what could only be described as a mixture of wonder and perplexion. What on earth was he going to say now?

"I'm planning to enjoy every part of you, Analisse Lejeune. Every inch and every flinch. So I'm only going to kiss you when the time is right.

Rossiter really was quite the wordsmith! The fact that she was incredibly turned on by now, whilst also feeling incredibly safe with him, meant that there was often a certain incongruity to the lascivious lothario's witty turn of phrase. The sound that escaped her mouth lay somewhere between a giggle and a gasp. How *dare* he talk like that? How *dare* he be so confident all the time? So irreverent? But that was such a big part of what had first attracted her to him, and continued to do so. Ana had had a few boyfriends in the past; some only brief liaisons, others longer term. But Rossiter was something of an unknown quantity, a *challenge*! The boys that she'd been with previously – and the more she thought about it, the more she realised that they really *were* mere boys – were in absolutely no way comparable to Clarke. He was a *man*, and she was going to enjoy allowing him to prove it to her.

Lying back on the bed, she rolled over and grabbed Clarke's shirt, pulling him towards her. She reached up and started undoing his buttons one by one, slowly, in a calculated manner, undressing him with purpose, until the shirt finally surrendered to her touch, and duly succumbed. She tossed it onto the bedroom floor.

He had a decent body. Not "ripped", like so many of the playboy, good looking guys that seemed to swarm the earth these days. Most fellas of Analisse´s age nowadays were all *Instagram, wham, bam, thank you mam*. But Clarke was different. Quite good looking, but not spectacular. But he was here, and he was *real*. He got rid of his socks, shoes, and trousers, and was now just a body – complete with just a little bit of a beer belly – and boxers. Black.

Despite his promise not to kiss Ana until the proverbial *point of no return*, Clarke was finding it increasingly difficult to keep his word. He drew her towards him, longing for her, before pushing her away playfully, but with intent. Rossiter ran the forefinger of his left hand from the top of Ana's right breast, gliding over the nipple with the faintest of touches, and leaving his digit there for just a split second, to gauge her reaction. Ana groaned, a whimper bordering on ecstasy. He knew that many women had extremely sensitive nipples, and Analisse seemed to be one of them. His touching of her left breast in the exact same way – and her identical reaction – appeared to indicate that her little pink points were indeed sensitive souls. Rossiter ran his tongue over the left one, before enclosing his teeth around it and giving the faintest of bites. It was playful, and not in any way intended to be violent. An act more delicious than malicious. He then moved back to the right breast, squeezing the end between thumb and forefinger.

"that feels so good..."

"Do you want me to stop?"

"Don't you daaaaare..."

Clarke kissed that most sublime of necks again, as his hot, heavy breathing into her ear caused Ana to arch her whole body backwards. No man had *ever* touched or talked to her the way Clarke was daring to. She'd never felt like this; it was as though Rossiter held some sort of power over her that was almost bordering on the supernatural. He seemed so in control, and Ana was *losing* hers. It was disconcerting, maybe even a little bit dangerous. She was feeling almost powerless - and she *loved* it!

Rossiter's hands glided downwards, caressing Analisse's belly and duly heading south. He pushed her lightly back onto the bed, and for the very first time ran the index and middle finger of his right hand over her knickers. Red and ready; the door to the promised land...

As he lightly rubbed again, adding a thumb this time, she moaned. Ana was renowned for her "prises de tête", as Clarke would later find out. But this was an altogether different kind of moan; one of ecstasy, expectation. Rossiter went back to Ana's left ear, and whispered, teasingly, almost mockingly:

"It seems like my naughty little Frenchy´s enjoying herself", he said, rubbing again, a little harder this time, but still outside her undergarments. Then, in the midst of Analisse's excitement, Rossiter took his hand away, and looked at her lying on the bed, eyes expectantly looking back at him. She couldn't take much more, such was the pocket rocket from Pélissanne's state of arousal.

No man has ever spoken to me, touched me or turned me on like this, Ana thought to herself as Clarke was talking. He was teasing her. W*as she just his new toy? If that's all she was, then she fucking liked it.*

But Ana was getting tired of his talking. She pushed both hands down, and tore her red underwear off with fervour, with such relish, as to leave the ravenous Rossiter in no doubt as to what she wanted. There she was, lying naked, pure, beautiful. Ana was by nature a timid girl. But she was giving herself to Rossiter willingly, perhaps even wantonly, and it was supposed to be this way. They *both* knew it, both *wanted* it.

Clarke liked what he saw. She could see him smirking, she knew that he wanted her, that he was dying to delve into her depths. Rossiter smiled as his hands began to caress Ana's body once again. He ran his right hand down her flustered face, gliding an index finger over her cheek, before taking a detour, tracing her luscious pink lips. Ana's mouth opened, she thought involuntarily, but Rossiter took it as a sign to embark upon the next phase of the journey. The next step.

Ana took his hand in her own, guiding it downwards. Clarke ran his hand over her breasts, before tracing her belly and delaying slightly, before arriving at the promised land.
He was teasing her. It was like torture for Ana, but in the best way imaginable. And Rossiter *knew* it.

He moved two fingers just above the proverbial box of treasures and began caressing the inside of each thigh, intentionally and agonisingly delaying. Becoming increasingly frustrated, Analisse decided to move her own right hand downwards. But this attempt proved to be in vain, as Clarke moved both of Ana's hands away from her thus far neglected nether regions. He did so with his by now familiar air of authority and control:

"Be patient, baby. It won't be long now..."

Having been thwarted in her attempts to do the work herself, Analisse attempted to take Clarke's hand and guide it to where she wanted it to go. But again, he stopped, looking her in the eye with a smirk that told her all she needed to know. He was playing with her, merely delaying the inevitable.

And then, finally, it happened. Rossiter duly delved down below, locating a thin line that had often been referred to as a "landing strip" during Clarke's younger day. Whether that expression for a narrow expanse of pubic sprouting was still *de rigueur* in this day and age, he had absolutely no idea.

Rossiter absolutely *never* got nervous around women; not even the most jaw droppingly, bona fide beautiful ones. Funnily enough, the more beautiful the girl was, the *less* trouble Clarke usually had in approaching, talking to, seducing and sleeping with her. It has often been said that *for every beautiful girl, there's a guy who's bored of fucking her...* This is what 99% of men fail to realise: because they are automatically turned on by a woman's *physical* attributes – initially at least - the male brain attributes excessive importance to a woman´s beauty, primarily by virtue of how they *look*. Other factors may or may not subsequently come into play. But, as stated previously, men's attraction stimuli are almost always *physical*, as opposed to those of most women being primarily triggered by feelings and *emotions*.

Hence, when the vast majority of men enter a bar, a club, or any other *seduction venue*, they will automatically notice the most physically attractive women. However, most of them will subsequently either lack the courage to even approach them, or mess things up when they do. This is usually because they (men) either get too nervous, or they try too hard. Male psychology dictates that we place beautiful women on a metaphorical pedestal because of how they *look*. As a consequence, the majority of men automatically assume that just because a woman is good looking, she's inherently "too good" for him. Most guys never even consider that because very attractive ladies often intimidate most men (intentionally or otherwise), and because most men are scared to even approach them, this means that very cute women are often alone at bars not because they think they're "too good" for any guy, but because most men don't dare to even *try* and talk to them. Consequently, they are often bored, or even *lonely*. Rossiter understood this, and by talking to almost every woman he found attractive, he often reaped the rewards.

Therefore, Analisse Lejeune held absolutely no fears for Congletown's favourite conquistador. She was exceptionally attractive, and she maybe even made him feel slightly more nervous than he ordinarily would, but he was looking forward to getting to know her better in every conceivable way. Tonight would hopefully be just the beginning.

Clarke kissed Ana's neck as he continued to explore her. It was as though he were being granted permission to enter a new realm. As she continued to moan, writhe, almost convulse in ecstasy, Rossiter could tell that mademoiselle Lejeune was nearing the point of no return. He'd always enjoyed making women climax. Not only did Clarke enjoy the sexual act itself, but he absolutely adored giving pleasure to the numerous women he chose to be with. Of course, his own gratification was important too; but the act of providing a woman with so much pleasure contented him and turned him on almost immeasurably.

"You're nearly there, baby", Clarke said as his magic digits did their work, before being replaced by his tongue. She looked, smelled and tasted so good; Rossiter wanted to devour her "lady flower". As he continued to pleasure her, Rossiter looked once again at Ana's face, as she neared a climax of almost religious proportions.

She arched her back, before letting out an almost animalistic cry. True to his word, at the exact moment that Ana reached her knee-trembling nirvana, Clarke looked her straight in the eye, with a look that said he wanted to *devour* her, and as her eyes rolled back into her head, he kissed her for the very first time. Contrary to Rossiter's firm and forthright fingers, the kiss was soft, slow, measured, delicate, full of passion and longing, his lips almost massaging hers as a prelude to him introducing just a hint of tongue. It was like no other kiss that either of them had ever experienced before; if desire had a voice, it was speaking to them now.

Still shaking, Analisse took a deep breath, still trying to take in what had just happened. Clarke pulled her towards him, kissed her again, more quickly and powerfully this time, reaching for a condom as he did so. The professor kissed Ana again, and slid inside, putting his arms around her narrow, slim waist and proceeding to pull her in towards him.

"If I'm hurting you, or if you don't like something, just let me know... ok?"

"Yeah..."

Clarke arched his back slightly, and continued at his rhythm. From the flustered Frenchy's reaction, it seemed as though she was enjoying it. Clarke was powerful and in control, but not in a bad way. He wasn't particularly well endowed, but seemed to know exactly how to use what God had given him.

After around twenty – five minutes - Rossiter was not a machine – he could feel he was almost ready. The professor only needed a few more seconds before the deed was done. Clarke climaxed with a satisfied, masculine moan, before leaning over and kissing Analisse again, that most carnal of acts complete.

7.

It was 10 am when Rossiter woke. He was still a little bit groggy, but turning over, the smile returned as he laid eyes on Ana, on her side, still sleeping. She was lying motionless, breathing so softly as to be almost inaudible, her light breaths in and out rhythmically punctuating the serene silence that cloaked the new lovers. She was the embodiment of peaceful perfection. The sheets hid her right breast, but the left lay uncovered, presenting itself to him like a magnificent monument; a fabulous momento of last night's escapades.

In the past, it had always amused Clarke to hear or read members of both sexes (but especially women) talking about their sexual exploits with such hyperbole, as though the animalistic exchange of bodily fluids were something so precious and special as to have been almost heaven sent, when in reality, the combination of sexual organs and *walk of shame Morgens* usually amounted to little more than a fleshy Fandango of lust and libido. As he contemplated Ana lying next to him, however, he now understood – at least in part – the motivation behind and justification for such sappy, overly sentimental idealising of what was essentially a wholly normal, everyday act; the mere coming together of two individuals in order to satisfy the laws of nature. Rossiter was often cynical, but last night and this morning's sleepy aftermath had apparently awoken emotions within him that he'd never felt before. Lying there facing him only a matter of inches away, Ana was beautiful, absolutely magnificent, in fact. Her young, almost childlike face with just a hint of pink in the cheeks as she continued to dream – maybe of him – was peaceful, precious, and as close to perfect as he could ever dare himself to admit. Clarke had watched scores of women sleeping the morning after their having been granted access into his bed, usually contemplating them with a mixture of mild amusement and disinterest, giving the latest conne-quest the usual spiel about how much fun it had been, before they invariably went their separate ways. As his eyes remained upon Analisse, however, Rossiter *knew* it was different this time.

He was *falling* for her.

8.

Clarke ran his hand along Ana's back with a tenderness which had heretofore always been totally alien to him. Although he had loved and respected women for as long as he could remember, and had always adored being in their company, prior to meeting Analisse, his attitude – towards women and life in general – had always been never to take them (or it) too seriously, and just to enjoy everything, whatever choices he made. But after last night's game of seduction and the mind – blowing sex that had followed, he felt that these were unchartered waters. It was always totally unknown territory once feelings threatened to enter the fray. Rossiter had always tried to avoid having feelings for women, or any possibility of them developing. But as he slid out of bed and looked back at the sleeping beauty over his shoulder upon leaving the bedroom, he surprisingly felt no fear with regard to any potential feelings developing towards her. *La Frenchy fantastique* was threatening to awaken something in Clarke that had thus far lain dormant, and rather than running scared, he wanted to embrace it and see where this new, unknown road might lead.

Rossiter slipped quietly out of the boudoir and headed into the kitchen. He made a strong coffee for himself, and a cup of tea and a plate of scrambled eggs for Ana. She'd mentioned in passing that this was her preferred breakfast whenever she could summon the energy to make it for herself. As she was still resting, Clarke took it upon himself to prepare it for her. It'd be a welcome surprise, and also an energy boost to make up for some of the calories lost in battle the previous night. Who knew, maybe some sustenance would set things up nicely for round two, fingers crossed.

With breakfast now cooked and tea perfectly brewed, Clarke made his way back to the bedroom, and placed Ana's tray down on the bedside table next to her. Despite his best attempts to do so quietly, putting the tray down caused a slight tapping sound, and duly woke Analisse up.

"Morning sleepy head!"

"Ohhh....heeey you! What time is it?"

"Nearly 10:30. But I didn't want to wake you earlier. You were out like a light! Obviously needed your beauty sleep..." he retorted with a wink and trademark cheeky grin.

"Haha! Cheeky sod! And what might *this* be?!"

"I made you breakfast. I remember you once said you were quite partial to scrambled eggs and a cup of tea to kick-start your day! So I made your favourite petit déjeuner, just for you!"

"Awww. And you even remembered that I take my tea with milk. English style!"

"Of course! Is there any *other* way to partake of England's favourite hot beverage?!"

"Haha, no! This is perfect! I'm starting to think you, Mr. Rossiter, might be a keeper! Play your cards right, and I might just have a nice little morning surprise for *you*..." she said with a wink, and that most sexy of smiles. The fact that she'd only just returned to the land of the living and was still sleepy, made it all the more cute. Ana took her tea from the tray, raising the china to her lips and taking a sip. Her beautiful face, still tired and not yet ready to face the day ahead, bore a striking resemblance to the cup from which she drank; clean, white, pure, and *hot*.

Clarke sat down next to Ana on the bed, leaning across to kiss her as she lay. She took another sip of tea, almost burning her luscious lips in doing so, and looked across at Clarke. He smiled, giving her a playfully mischievous slap on the behind, and gestured towards the plate:

"Don't let those eggs get cold, missy! Such delightful morning treats will give you energy for round two! And it should also be noted that I don't usually make breakfast for girls. Or anyone, for that matter. So come on, eat up! An egg a day, makes Ana want to play..."

She looked up at Clarke with feigned annoyance, tutted, and went back to the eggs, which she found almost as delicious as he who had prepared them. She would devour Rossiter (again) later. But first she had to fill her stomach.

Replete, and with plate now empty, Ana turned over onto her side and looked at Clarke:

"Come on, loverboy! What are you waiting for?"

He couldn't wait any longer; round two was mere moments away...

9.

Rossiter looked over at Ana, asleep once again. She lay on her left side, hair dishevelled, with a slight breeze from the open bedroom window blowing it over the pillow in the aftermath of what had been *quite* the matinée performance. Her beautiful naked body was facing him, unobstructed by sheets this time, perhaps as testament to the fact that after this – the second round of how's your father – she was slowly but surely becoming more comfortable in his presence, so much so, that bare flesh was now something that she no longer felt the need to cover within the confines of a satin safeguard.

Clarke afforded himself a satisfied smile and went to make more coffee, deciding to let her repose a while longer in the post-coital afterglow. He slipped out of bed with weary satisfaction, and went straight to the kitchen.

Analisse was really starting to intrigue Rossiter, almost to the point of fascination. Yes, the sex was great, in spite of their physical limitations. But there was more to her than that. Granted, there hadn't been much cause for conversation over the last few hours. But when they *had* talked, he found that there was so much more to her than great boobs and brown hair. She appeared not to be entirely comfortable with her disability. He already knew that. But he supposed that as they got to know each other better and she became more comfortable in his company, it might become less of a taboo. Such a theory was thus far proving incorrect, however. Ana still seemed to be extremely guarded, and reluctant to discuss the subject. Hence, Clarke had chosen not to push it. She would talk when she felt ready. The other thing that was starting to puzzle him slightly, was the fact that she had yet to mention what she did. She'd never mentioned a job or studies, even when Clarke had hinted at wanting to find out more about her in a professional sense. He was interested in her background and what she may or may not be doing with her life, but it wasn't a deal breaker. In truth, he never particularly cared about what the innumerable women in his life dedicated their time to. The fact that he was more preoccupied with Ana than he had ever been with any other démoiselle found Rossiter questioning himself more than he may have liked to. There would be plenty of time to ponder such matters, however.

    Clarke picked up his coffee and wandered back into the bedroom. Analisse was now stirring, stifling a yawn and seemingly ready to get up. She threw the covers off, and swung her legs over the side of the bed, stretching her arms heavenward as she did so, yawning once more.

"Oh, hey Clarke."

"Hi. I brought you another cup of tea. Springton´s. It's a really great local brand. There's a fella who sells it door to door. Myself and my stepfather swear by it!"

"Oh, thanks, but I really have to go now..."

"Seriously? Most of the ladies to come here never normally get so much as a coffee and a goodbye cuddle! So for you to have earned not one, but *two* cups of tea would appear to confirm your status as quite the welcome guest, ma lady..."

Ana proffered an apologetic movement of the lips that could barely be deemed a smile, quickly getting dressed and looking guiltily back at him, before confirming her apparent desire to vacate the premises:

"No, I really should get going. It's been great catching up, but I've got stuff I need to be doing. It's been fun. I'll call you..."

And she left, scuttling towards the door in an attempt to abscond as quickly as possible, mustering only a half hearted wave of her right hand as she closed the front door behind her, leaving a puzzled Rossiter in her wake.

There was more to this girl, and more to this story, than met the eye...

10.

Clarke walked away from the (now firmly closed) front door. He was confused, but still managed to smile to himself as he mused over the fact that women, apparently, were like doors; wide open and welcoming when the good times were in the offing, only to be slammed shut and bound under proverbial lock and key once the hanky panky and subsequent small talk were complete. Rossiter acknowledged the fact that they had had a good time together, only for her legs and the door to have slammed firmly shut once the deed were done. Clarke, of course, was no stranger to the whys, wherefores and whims of the female of the species. He was perfectly aware that many women chose to vanish following a night of passion, rather than indulge in the forced pleasantries of the morning after. But Ana hadn't seemed like that kind of girl. Sure, she was cute; they all were. Rossiter wouldn't entertain spending time with anyone who wasn't. He had never made any apologies for that, or attempted to justify his reasons for such behaviour. He loved beautiful women, and that was all the justification he needed.

Analisse Lejeune had seemed different, however. Yes, the sex had been absolutely spectacular. And they'd appeared to have made quite the *connection* – a word often overused and exaggerated by the love starved sad sacks of the modern world – but it was certainly true in this case. Girls like that didn't just leave for no reason, and Rossiter was determined to find out quite why she had chosen to depart so hastily…

11.

He went back to lie down on the bed, reasoning that another hour's sleep couldn't hurt. When he eventually awoke it was 2 pm, but the tardy hour gave him little to no cause for concern.
Clarke went to the kitchen, debating whether to opt for another coffee, or an early afternoon beer. Caffeine would win... for now.

Sitting and sipping, his mind returned to the events of the previous night and following morning; the Analisse dilemma. It – and indeed she – was turning into quite the head scratching post – coital conundrum. Rossiter wasn't normally one for over-thinking things with regard to women. Or anything, for that matter. But her precipitated exit that morning had left him with more questions than answers, and he desired to get to the bottom of it. He wouldn't call her, however. That was a fool's errand. And Clarke Rossiter was many things, but a fool could never be listed among them. His shortcomings were numerous, but he would refrain from dialling her number.

After a considerable period of deliberation, he decided to take his usual course of action when choosing whether or not to reconnect with a dame with whom he had dallied; no action at all. Yes, Ana had certainly left her mark upon Rossiter. But if she chose to contact him again, that would be *her* decision. Clarke loved women, but absolutely never *chased* them, and as such, the ball was now firmly in the Frenchy's court. Rather like a game at Snoland Farros. *New balls, please.*

12.

It was Friday night again. Clarke arrived home from yet another energy – sapping and somewhat tedious day at work which had been strikingly similar to the preceding ones. The new school year at Congletown University was due to begin on the following Monday, and with all of the necessary bureaucracy and preparation now complete, this would be Rossiter's final weekend of relaxation before returning to academia in three days' time.

It was 6:30 pm by the time the front door swung open and he walked into the hall, dumping bag and jacket on the table and subsequently stifling a yawn. After yet another day surrounded by pontificating, pretentious professors, the only company Clarke wished to be in now, was that of beer or wine. Walking wearily into the kitchen and glancing at a sink full of dishes that he had absolutely *no* intention of washing for the foreseeable, he negotiated a stray chair that was strewn across the room, before stumbling to the drinks cupboard to choose his weapon of choice. He opted for a Mendoza Malbec, withdrawing one of the few remaining clean glasses and filling said receptacle with an ample serving of fine,

Argentinian claret.

In the early evening sunshine, Rossiter sat on the *bandstand* and sipped. He immediately began to feel more relaxed as the fruity red entered his mouth and caressed the back of his throat. It was approaching seven pm, and the mid September sun was still pleasantly warm, as was always the case at that time of year. Clarke felt extremely grateful to be living in such a fantastic part of the world.

Putting his glass down, the professor looked across the yard, squinting and shielding his eyes, having previously forgotten to pick up his sunglasses from the kitchen upon pouring the wine. As he looked beyond the wall at the far end of his private terrace, a delightful sight greeted him. A girl was standing on the opposite balcony, attempting to dry her seemingly damp hair in the early evening sunshine. The lady in question – a new neighbour, presumably – had obviously just climbed out of her private pool, as drops of water glistened on her golden torso, shrouded in a crisp white bikini, with the glint of sunshine adding a seductive sparkle to both skin and swimwear. Although Clarke was a considerable distance away, the newcomer appeared quite tall, and looked to be in either her late twenties or perhaps early thirties. She took a towel from off the deck, and proceeded to tousle her long, dark hair. Rossiter was thus far unsure whether it was brown or black. Her skin was extremely tanned; a colour resembling caramel that shimmered and shone as she dried off in the warm evening air. She looked Spanish, or possibly South American. Having tossed the towel aside, she turned and looked across the terrace to see Rossiter standing with cane in left hand and vino in right. He looked directly at her, raising his glass as a smile of amused anticipation edged across his lips.

"Howdy, neighbour! I don't believe we've met. I'm Clarke, and *you* are sublime! Who might you be?"

"Hello Clarke. I'm Lexi. Pleased to meet you! I'm new to these parts, so I need to know what this neighbourhood is all about. You're not one of the resident troublemakers, are you?"

"Well now, that'd be telling! But for *you*, sexy Lexi, I promise to be on my best behaviour. Will you come and join me for a drink? It *is* the weekend, after all…"

Within five minutes, the new neighbours had become officially acquainted, lying next to one another on the sun loungers that Congletown's most eligible bachelor rarely had cause to use. Lexi Faloma had brought her own towel, and still wore the dazzling white bikini which Rossiter had been only too happy to feast his eyes upon mere moments earlier. Having poured two glasses of chilled New Zealand Sauvignon blanc, he turned to watch her as she sipped, stretching out on the sunbed in a mirage of bikini clad magnificence. Lexi's beautiful sun dappled skin meant that Clarke's eyes couldn't fail to be drawn to her as she talked:

"I'm originally from Lima, the capital of Peru, but I've been living in this country for the last few years, and have just moved here, to the city I mean. So these parts are all totally new to me. Who knows, maybe you'd like to be my tour guide? I need someone to show me around."

"Sure. I know a few places."

"I should warn you though, I have very little free time these days. I

found a new job, which was actually the reason I moved here, so that takes up all of my time. Hence my not having had time to visit the city."
Rossiter nodded, taking on board this new information along with a refreshing sip of white wine.

"What is it that you do, Lexi? I presume your profession must be something you're passionate about, given that you appear to dedicate so much time to it."

"I'm a waitress at one of the best restaurants in the city. It's out on the marina. I'm there fifteen hours a day, and it's exhausting sometimes. But I love what I do!"

She raised her glass in her interlocutor's direction, with a beaming smile. It was one of the heartiest, fullest, most friendly smiles Clarke had ever seen. The kind of smile that instantly made any person warm to her and want to find out more. The fact that she also had such an incredible body wasn't lost on Rossiter, and would entice any man worthy of the name.
Sexy Lexi appeared to be quite the temptress.

Seeing that the latest in his ever lengthening line of cute drinking partners had finished her first glass, Rossiter took the bottle of white from the ice bucket, and poured Lexi another one. As they continued chatting, she went on to tell him – amidst all the other inconsequential small talk – that she was 28 years old, and lived with her cousin, who was out with friends for the night, and apparently quite the party animal. Lexi's parents were both back in Peru, along with her two sisters. She was the middle child, and as the conversation progressed, Clarke was surprised that the *pearl from Peru* never again mentioned her siblings.

The remainder of Rossiter and Lexi's first ever conversation told how she'd left Lima at a relatively young age to study in Europe and fulfill her dream of working in the hospitality trade. Her hand had been forced somewhat, owing to the lack of work back home, and she'd found herself embarking upon a journey to foreign shores and subsequently to Congletown, despite still being in her twenties. Aside from the fact that she was absolutely beautiful – Rossiter loved Hispanic and South American women – there was just something warm and caring about Latina ladies that was often absent in English or other European girls, and Lexi was the same. However, what he most admired about her was the fact that she worked hard, had goals and ambitions, and had fought incredibly hard to achieve them. Sure, Clarke enjoyed casual drinking and one nighters with party girl types, but only very occasionally, these days. In fact, as he was now in his thirties, he was starting to get bored of girls with no substance, drive or ambition. On the increasingly rare occasions that he spent an evening or night with those he referred to as *Instagram girls or copy and paste cuties*, he seldom called or saw them again. Rossiter was slowly realising that although drinks and casual sex were often fun, he was beginning to feel that he wanted and needed more connection, more of a *genuine* kind of intimacy and depth to the friendships and relationships he now chose to pursue. That wasn't to say that he wouldn't continue to meet and sleep with beautiful women. But they now needed to have something more in their armoury than that which was merely physical. With age came great wisdom; Clarke would henceforth endeavour to actually get to know any woman he was interested in, rather than merely attempt to get them between the sheets, as had previously been his main aim with the dames. Sexy Lexi was sensational, with that wonderful smile, and beautiful brown eyes that could stir the soul of a dead man. But Clarke wanted to get to know her properly.

Even in their relatively brief opening exchanges, she'd made a good impression. She intrigued him, and he was eager to delve a little deeper in an attempt to find out more.

The time was now approaching eight pm. Both Clarke and Lexi finished their second glass of wine, and she got up off the sunbed to collect her few belongings. What she said next surprised him somewhat:

"Would you like to join me for dinner? I'd planned to try a new twist on a recipe for a dish I've been meaning to make for a while. I'm only a waitress, but I'm not too bad a cook, either. I've got all the ingredients, so there'll be more than enough for two. You're more than welcome, Professor!"

"Oh… thanks for the invite, but I'm afraid I'll have to decline. As delightful as an impromptu evening in your home cooking company sounds, I promised I'd call my mother before heading out this evening. She would doubtless be somewhat irked if I failed to comply. But another time, for sure!"

Family was very important to Rossiter, and he and his mother Linda had always been especially close. Clarke was genuine in his desire to get to know Lexi better, but he was also always wary of these situations, where dinner and drinks usually led to more. And although the professor's fascination with beautiful women was unlikely ever to change, tonight's unexpected meeting with the new neighbour had given him cause to re-evaluate a few things. Clarke decided that he would take the time to *really* get to know Lexi, rather than just try and get her into bed.

Yes, she intrigued him. But family and friends would always be more important to Rossiter than any woman.

As the *pearl from Peru* waved goodbye, surprised that the professor had declined her invite, but also pleased to have been in the company of a man who valued his nearest and dearest above all else, Clarke finished a last sip of wine, and walked inside to call his mother.

Linda was a senior radiographer with over thirty years' experience in her field, having worked both in public and private hospitals during the course of her career. She still loved her work, even after so many years of taking x – rays for the walking wounded. She had on occasion told Clarke that her only minor regret had been not making the decision to become a doctor, a position that she'd always believed herself capable of, had she decided to push herself even further. In spite of this, her work as a radiographer had always been such a fundamental part of her life and who she was, and she would continue to help people in the remaining time that she intended to stay in the job, and beyond.

Linda and Clarke had always been very close. Rossiter not only loved his mother dearly, but he admired and respected her for the dedicated, hard-working, kind and loving person that she was. Nothing was ever too much trouble, and she would always go out of her way to help anyone in any way she could. Along with his father and other close family members, Clarke's mum had always brought him up to be polite, respectful, and honest, values that she had herself chosen to live by.

Linda, like her second son, had endured a lot of hardship in her life, but had always come out the other side. She was determined, dedicated, and a real fighter. The fact that Clarke was almost always smiling, with a never say die attitude that had helped him to make a success of his young life, despite its inauspicious beginnings, was thanks in no small part to his mother's influence, values, and unwavering support and belief in him. Even when life was difficult for Rossiter, he never lost sight of the fact that he owed his family and friends a huge debt of gratitude for everything he had achieved against all the odds, and nobody more so than his mum.

The ensuing phone call was much like the others between Clarke and Linda. Having lived away from friends and family at various times in his life, Rossiter always made sure that he maintained regular contact with the people closest to him. There was absolutely no excuse *not* to these days, either by phone, video calls, or the advent of various forms of social media. Given that he disliked the modern world's dependence upon such means of communication, a good old fashioned chat on the phone was the professor's preferred way of catching up with those he chose to be in contact with.

As a general rule, he rang his mother twice a week, with calls tending to last around an hour, depending on how busy they both were. They always made time for each other, however, and tonight was no different. He proceeded to chat with Linda for the usual sixty minutes, making small talk about how everybody was, work, social events, all the usual subject matter normally covered in typical family phone calls. Linda had always been a massive influence on her son, a pillar of strength and fountain of wisdom, especially on the (albeit infrequent) occasions that life proved tough for Congletown's lovable lothario.

Having ascertained that all was well with his nearest and dearest, Clarke bade farewell to his mum, before setting the receiver down and heading into the kitchen in search of pre – Playhouse sustenance and further liquid refreshment.

He sipped casually on what would be his final glass of wine before heading to the bar. Given that this weekend would be his last stress – free one before Congletown University reopened its gates on Monday, Rossiter was fully intent on making the most of it.

The visit to the Playhouse was remarkably similar to all the others. He only ended up staying for around two hours, as was usually the case, regardless of whether he made the acquaintance of any new women or not. There weren't any noteworthy nubiles on this particular evening, save for the two new barmaids recently recruited to work alongside Rossiter's friend Beni Rothwell, both of whom were absolutely spectacular. He'd briefly chatted to both Carla and Hannah, and though both were beautiful, the former – an accountancy student, apparently – had left somewhat more of an impression on Rossiter. He would make an effort to converse with her again at a later date. But not tonight. He finished a third and final beer, before hauling his surprisingly weary frame out of the door, acknowledging Beni and the newcomers with a trademark wink and wave as he departed.

Saturday and Sunday followed much the same pattern as most other weekends; watching his beloved team before indulging in wine, cooking and subsequent devouring of said culinary creation.

Clarke wasn´t an outstanding chef. However, having moved around at a relatively young age to pursue his chosen course of studies and ensuing career path, he had already lived in different countries, despite his disability. Such life choices would potentially be difficult for any and *every* young person, regardless of any physical limitations. But by leaving his home in search of pastures new, despite his tender years, Clarke had been forced to grow up more quickly than most, and this involved learning everything from cooking and keeping house, to mastering new languages in an attempt to meet new people and adapt to new surroundings, with their inherent customs and cultures. Many young people would doubtless have found such changes daunting. For Rossiter, however, they were anything but. His mentality was such, that he saw this new direction he had chosen for his life to take not only as a journey – both figuratively *and literally* – but also an opportunity to test himself, and prove to himself and to others (not that he ever felt he *needed* to) that he could triumph in the face of doubt and adversity.

    The wine was going down a treat. Clarke´s friends from his time in France had introduced him to the culture of the apéritif – or *apéro* – which was particularly prevalent in the south. The custom of drinks prior to one´s evening meal remains a revered tradition in those parts, where a light snack and a glass of pastis, the local liquor enjoyed by friends, families and neighbours alike - as they endeavour to set the world to rights in that oh so Provençal way - is often the prelude to dinner time. Clarke had fond memories when reminiscing about his time in France, having attended many an animated apéro; with the singing cigales providing a buzzing backdrop to happy summer nights on many memorable occasions.

      Rossiter had been forced to do a lot of growing up during his time in France, and particularly in the first year. Although it seemed a long time ago now, he still regularly kept in touch with friends he'd made there. It – and they – would always be a hugely important part of his life. Moving away in one's twenties, to a new country, city, surroundings, language and people, had not only been an adventure, but also the catalyst for Clarke to evolve both personally and professionally. He had found out so much more about himself during that first year in the south of France, and it had been an unforgettable experience that he would cherish forever, even though some French people (his friends notwithstanding) annoyed him somewhat.

    There wasn't much to do on a Sunday night in Congletown. It was now almost ten, and having failed to find anything even remotely interesting to watch on TV, Clarke sought solace in another glass of wine. He'd considered asking Lexi to join him, but having only met her forty-eight hours previously, he surmised that inviting her over for drinks might appear too eager.

    Although Rossiter now had considerable success with the fairer sex, that hadn't always been the case. In his teens and even into his twenties, the professor had endured long periods of disappointment and frustration with women, thanks in no small part to his disability, the Cerebral Palsy that he'd had since birth.

A lifelong affliction.

Despite the fact that he'd always been extremely resilient, with high self-esteem and unwavering confidence in himself, Clarke had previously been convinced that although *he* believed that he was worthy of any woman he chose to be with, it was the girls who believed he wasn't good enough for *them*. A man or woman can be as confident and self-assured as he or she likes. But if the mere sight of a wheelchair or walking sticks causes a potential suitor's expression to change in the blink of an eye – and if it occurs repeatedly – then such a damning indictment may cause a person to question their attractiveness towards the opposite sex, regardless of how he or she views him or herself. Hence, Clarke Rossiter had always believed himself deserving of beautiful women, but he had always struggled to ensnare them. The professor had suffered countless rejections during his formative years of seduction, with literally every woman he'd ever been attracted to regrettably informing him that his feelings weren't reciprocated. They'd reeled out all the old chestnuts, such as not having time for a relationship, only looking for friendship, and on a couple of occasions when he'd conversed with new, unknown girls in bars, words hadn't even been necessary. As soon as his crutches had come into view, the girls' expressions always changed, as their smiles and clearly interested glances in his direction were replaced by a furrowing of the brow and a clear look of disappointment and even disapproval as it became apparent that Clarke had a disability. When they occur every once in a while, these rejections can be dealt with. But when it happens *all* the time, with *every* girl you're interested in, a man may begin to question his worth.

So he knew he had to rectify the situation, and he had. Rossiter still encountered disgruntled glances from women, and was occasionally rejected in his attempts to seduce them. But said rejections were now extremely infrequent, in stark contrast to the early years. He wasn't entirely sure what had changed. Probably the fact that he now viewed rejection as a learning process and something to build on, rather than the not inconsiderable stumbling block it had represented in his formative years. He no longer saw a turn of the head as a personal sleight, but rather something that all men and women experienced sometimes, and for any number of different reasons. Through experience, Rossiter had learnt that many elements of seduction were akin to what happened in everyday life: you have success and failure, and will make many mistakes along the way. The most important thing in life and love was to analyse your mistakes, find out where you went wrong, and learn from them in order to avoid a repeat in the future. Such advice was sometimes harder to apply in practice, but the notions held firm. Seduction isn't a science, rejection isn't (usually) personal, and adopting this mantra had allowed Clarke to rationalise the disappointments of the past, and subsequently become the unshakeably self – confident, though not arrogant, ladies' man he now was. But there would be none of that tonight. After a final fruitless search for something to watch, and one last glass of wine, Rossiter turned off the television, returned glass and bottle to the kitchen, and made his way to bed.

This was a school night.

13.

7 am. Alarm clock and hard cock. Rossiter slumped out of bed and wearily weaved his way to the bathroom to pee. He'd always hated Monday mornings – or *any* mornings for that matter – but this particular wake – up call heralded the first day of a new academic year at the University of Congletown. He would doubtless have to listen to all manner of bookwormy bollocks and pompous ramblings from both colleagues and students throughout the course of the day. The fact that this was the *first* day of the year, with teachers and pupils striving to regain their pretentious academic pomp, usually gave rise to an even greater level of bullshit than usual.

This thought appeared quite fitting as Rossiter sat down for his customary morning dump; his mind was much more on faeces than thesis. He hadn't even had time for coffee before taking to the throne. But with ablutions now complete, he ambled to the kitchen for a much needed mug of the nation's favourite hot beverage. Rossiter was never hungry at that time of the morning, but forced himself to have a meagre slice of toast as he sipped, contemplating a return to Congletown's hallowed halls after the summer hiatus, which was never long enough. Having forced down the toast and coffee, Clarke took a hot shower and went to get dressed, opting for a navy shirt, black suit and tie. He only ever wore a necktie on the first day of class, as a kind of symbolic gesture to avoid academia's noblesse from casting aspersions from atop their learned, lofty perch. Thereafter, any form of neckwear would be consigned to the back of a drawer, until such time as it be deemed necessary for various university functions such as staff / student drinks, conferences, graduations and the like.

It was approaching 8:15 as he set off to work, with the warm morning sun already bordering on hot. A jacket wasn't really necessary at this time of year, but the long summer break meant the professor was out of practice. Clarke always needed a few days at the start of a year or semester to get back into the swing of things. Lazy days and same night lays were now to be replaced by seminars and essay marking.
Welcome back to the wonderful world of academia, Professor Rossiter…

Clarke arrived at the university after the usual fifteen or twenty-minute walk, making his way up the steps and down the corridor to his office. Following a brief chat with Fina the cleaner, Rossiter sat down at the desk to do one final check of his lesson plan – if you could call it that – in preparation for the students' arrival. Everything appeared to be in order, apart from the secretary having failed to provide him with class lists for the new groups of students, which was par for the course, given the incompetency of the administrative staff at Congletown. There was so much nonsense and needless bureaucracy woven into the very fabric of the institution, coupled with the majority of the office staff who barely had a brain cell between them, let alone a degree, that it was a wonder anything ever got done.

Rossiter sighed, leaning back in his chair to wait for the students. Class was due to start in under five minutes.

Welcome back, Clarkey boy!

      The professor stifled a yawn, and was interrupted in doing so by a knock on the office door that was so quiet as to be almost inaudible. He waited, smiling to himself as he imagined his new charges behind the door. Whoever had knocked had done so with such timidity, that he had hardly even heard them do so. Clarke remembered his own university days, those first forays into academia, where naivety reigned. The difference between secondary school and university was considerable. Leaving home at eighteen, to a new city where you didn´t know anybody, was certainly daunting. But Rossiter had embraced that particular challenge in much the same way as he had done all the others in his life. Yes, he had been nervous, as anybody would have been when leaving home, abandoning your comfort zone and everything you´ve ever known, to embark upon the journey into further education. These young kids behind the office door were about to become not only students, but adults too. Rossiter smiled nostalgically as he remembered his first tentative steps into that new environment. It had been a daunting yet exciting journey, one that the new students were about to undertake.

A second knock

  "Come in!"

      The door creaked slightly and slowly crept open. Rossiter smiled warmly at the swathes of students – of whom there appeared to be about forty – as they nervously made their way to a seat, muttering a collective hello as they did so.

  "Good morning, ladies and gentlemen! I am Professor Clarke Rossiter.

You can call me Professor, Mister Rossiter, even Clarke, should you so desire. Call me anything… as long as it's respectful and appropriate in these hallowed halls, a place of learning! Welcome to Congletown University!"

Given that some students were still clambering through the door and attempting to find a seat, Clarke had yet to see all of them, so vast were the numbers. It was the same every year, with huge numbers of students signing up to his classes, which meant that around forty or even fifty started the semester, cramped into Rossiter's office, which was designed to accommodate twenty-five, thirty at most. Proof of yet another administrative oversight that the office staff made year after year, but never corrected. Some students quit the course after the first couple of weeks, so numbers were invariably reduced somewhat. But having so many bodies in such a confined space could never be conducive to learning.

With all the new, first – year students now seated, Rossiter glanced down at his lesson plan, musing over exactly how to begin the class. Still looking at the paper, he distractedly pointed – without even looking – at the first person on the front row:

"Would you like to close the door, please?"

With eyes still fixed on his hastily scribbled notes, the professor heard the shuffling of feet and the door closing. He looked up to see which student had done so, and his heart skipped a beat.

His new student was none other than Analisse Lejeune…

14.

He hadn´t been expecting that!

Rossiter stood before the class, doing his utmost to remain calm and focused in front of his new charges. It promised to be an arduous task, given the bombshell that had just exploded. Ana was here, in Clarke´s Congletown classroom, and the professor was struggling to hold it together. He was normally so calm, composed and in control of his emotions. But miss Lejeune showing up here had really thrown the chatte amongst the proverbial pigeons. In the grand scheme of things, it shouldn´t actually have been so much of a surprise; they´d only ever had brief conversations about their professional lives, and Analisse had hinted at forays into academia. But her being a student had only ever been implied, and never confirmed. It hadn´t appeared to be particularly important to either of them when they´d met and subsequently got to know one another, with student life a mere anecdote in their burgeoning tale of nocturnal meets and soiled sheets. And now here she was, back in Rossiter´s life after several months of no news. Clarke had somewhat begrudgingly attempted to contact her on a couple of occasions since their last meeting which had ended so bizarrely, but to no avail. He´d frequently found himself thinking about her, much more so than he usually did with any girl he slept with. He wanted to try to rationalise the situation and get to the bottom of exactly why she´d chosen to end it so abruptly, and seemingly without just cause. But alas, after all that time with not so much as a whisper from her, he'd decided to let it go.

Or that's what would've happened in an ideal world, at least.

Still endeavouring to keep his cool, Clarke addressed the class once more:

"This is our first class together. Your first taste of higher education, and the first step on a road strewn with countless obstacles for you to overcome and challenges for you all to face. You have chosen to study English Literature. This is a journey down a difficult road; a road that will lead you either to literary greatness… or to the job centre."

Laughter.

"So with that in mind, before we delve into the literary canon and all of its inherent delights, I will ask you a question:

Why? Why are you here this morning? Why did you choose this course? Why do you want to study literature?"

Rossiter paused, shifting his focus to Analisse Lejeune, and with his eyes fixed on her, staring directly at her, he repeated:

"Why?

Why?

Why?"

15.

Ana stared straight back at the professor, *her* new professor, trying as hard as she possibly could to keep her cool. *Garder le sang froid* was such a clichéd expression in French, her native tongue, but never before had it seemed so apt. As the steely, unerring stare of Clarke's brown eyes not only looked back at her, but somehow seemed to bore a hole right into the depths of her very soul, Analisse Lejeune's blood ran icy cold...

Rossiter addressed the students once again, finally allowing Ana to look away, as she'd been dying to do all along. She instinctively angled her blue / green eyes down to her notebook, owing to the fact that she had few other options of where to focus her gaze. Her nerves were destroyed; looking at Rossiter again just wasn't an option. It would be more than she could take. How could she – and indeed they – have ended up in this situation? Yes, Analisse recalled Clarke talking very briefly about his working life: there had been brief mention of him being a teacher, along with fleeting reference to occasional writing projects, about which he had divulged almost nothing. Ana herself had only hinted at the fact that she had an academic background, without ever going into any detail whatsoever about what she studied, or indeed where. So while it were true that Congletown wasn't a particularly big place, she hadn't expected for their paths to cross again in these circumstances, and she supposed that Clarke hadn't, either.

As Rossiter had stared at her earlier, she'd felt that his asking the class about their motivation for studying literature – and his unmistakably forthright repetition of the word *why* – had served as little more than a premise for him to also question her about quite why she had left so hurriedly the previous time they'd met. Yes, Ana often had a tendency to overthink and analyse things; but despite the way he'd looked at her, wishing to showcase his confidence through that trademark strong eye contact, the vulnerability was also clear as he looked over towards his most unexpected of new students. The way he stared at her, it was as though Rossiter were imploring her to provide the answers that he had thus far failed to find.

But what would they be?

16.

With the first class of a hectic new academic year over, Congletown University's newest recruits slinked out of Rossiter's office. The looks the students gave him as they exited the room – doubtless to seek solace in either a cup of coffee, or perhaps the welcoming arms of a supportive loved one – were varied. There had been several beaming smiles from the scores of cute girls whose faces shone with excitement and contentment at having taken their first steps into university life; satisfaction at a first rewarding foray into the adult world. Their naivety was delightful, striking a chord with Clarke as he momentarily reminisced about his own scholarly beginnings. University had been a wonderfully exciting time for the professor, and the mixture of excitement, trepidation and perhaps even sheer bemusement that he saw etched upon the students´ faces as they exited his arena caused him to force a nostalgic smile in memory of bygone days.

As he stooped to pick up his semblance of a lesson plan from the desk, along with numerous other administrative documents that were par for the course whenever Congletown reopened its gates, upon turning towards his office door in search of the staff room and a much needed caffeine refuel, Rossiter stopped upon hearing a questioning voice from outside:

"Professor... Rossiter? Clarke?"

Analisse.

Having shuffled the remaining papers into his bag, Rossiter made his way towards the office door, merely casting a questioning glance over his shoulder in an effort to ascertain exactly what Ana wanted. A question that had apparently fallen upon deaf ears.

"Clarke..."

Trying – probably in vain – not to appear or sound agitated, Clarke pivoted to face her:

"Ana... what do you want? I really don´t have time for this – whatever *this* is. Today of all days!"

"Can we... talk?"

"Well... unless you feel the need to pick my brains about the finer points of literature, I don´t really see that we have much to discuss. Any academic queries you may have can be discussed with any member of the study liaison staff. Good day, miss Lejeune."

17.

Rossiter´s words and their delivery hadn´t been particularly antagonistic or mean. It was just the way that he´d looked at her and spoken in a manner that was so matter-of-fact, composed, calculated, almost *neutral*, that had unsettled Ana; merely a teacher fulfilling his duties and adhering to a professional code of conduct. He appeared to be able to draw a line between his work and personal life, and adapt his behaviour accordingly. As he´d addressed her with abruptness and mild irritation following that first class, her new, unexpected mentor had seemed like a totally different man to the one who had delicately defiled her prior to their unanticipated academic re-acquaintance. Maybe their nights of passion had merely been a prologue to a story now doomed to fail. As they had lain together in the resplendent afterglow of their naked narrative, they had been equals – or so she´d thought. But now, in just a few brief seconds and the most unexpected of plot twists, the context had changed entirely. Professor Rossiter was the master, and Ana merely a student; the apparent victim of Congletown's very own geek tragedy...

The remainder of the professor's first day back at work passed off without any further dramas or surprises. Rossiter had students from every academic year at Congletown, from nervous first years taking their first steps on what would hopefully be a long and rewarding academic journey, right through to the Master's students for whom the scholarly pilgrimage was nearing its end. Clarke enjoyed teaching each age group for different reasons. Of course, every class had its mixture of timid teenagers, class clowns and sycophantic savants, and everything else in between. Perhaps unsurprisingly, he'd always preferred teaching the older students, as they were usually – though not always – more learned and experienced in both life *and* literature. Though there were occasional exceptions, the majority of first year students were often timid and lacking the courage of their convictions, due to university life still being so new to them. It was a step into the unknown; a journey that some learners were cut out for, others not.

Although Rossiter's work sometimes frustrated him, the thing he invariably enjoyed most was that irrespective of year group or class, there was always a wide range of students from a whole host of different social and academic backgrounds, and with varying levels of ability. As one of Congletown's longest serving staff members, Clarke now had many years' experience of imparting his knowledge to scores of learners. And while it were true that the vast majority merely chose to come to classes, study hard and earn a degree within the confines of relative academic anonymity, it occasionally came to pass – albeit very infrequently – that Rossiter encountered an individual of exceptionally high intellect. He was loathe to use the word *genius* in reference to such students; those rare beacons of bookwormy braininess shining bright amidst the sallow shade of their lesser gifted peers. When those rare learned lights *did* appear, however, Clarke found it extremely satisfying. Seeing an exceptionally talented learner progress and evolve was doubtless the most rewarding part of the job – student bodies in short skirts notwithstanding.

    Grabbing his jacket and briefcase from off the desk, Clarke left his office mere seconds after the final five o´clock class ended, stopping to drop off some paperwork in the staff room before heading home in the afternoon sun. Having been sitting down for the vast majority of the day, save for an occasional walk to the board to draw the students´ attention to something, Clarke found that he was always appreciative of the walk home, especially at this time of year when the sun was still warm. After this, the first day back, the perambulation would give Rossiter time to muse over everything that had happened... and also to think about the fact that Analisse Lejeune had so unexpectedly reappeared in his life.

    This unwelcome development presented something of a conundrum. Ordinarily, Clarke had absolutely no difficulty in choosing to cut contact with girls who became boring, either because they were forever complaining, placing unreasonable demands on him, or because he decided that things with any particular woman had – as he always told them – merely run their course. Despite his intentions always being to *let the girl down gently*, such assertions in a parting of the ways invariably culminated in the casting of aspersions and insults being hurled towards him, sometimes punctuated by screaming and intermittent sobs from the countless cuties that the carefree Clarke chose to cast aside.

That was the thing: it was always a choice. *His* choice. Having fared so poorly with the opposite sex during his teenage years and early adulthood, he had long since decided that having become a master of seduction as the years progressed, things would be done on *his* terms, and no-one else's. This wasn't because the professor intended to be mean or insensitive to any girl's feelings; it was just that he had been messed around by so many of them in the past, and wasted so much time with women who weren't worth his time, but he had just taken too long to realise it and assert himself. No, Clarke wasn't mean – not intentionally, anyway – just honest and direct in setting boundaries for women and telling them exactly what he wanted. If any particular damsel in distress didn't like it, then so be it. *Ruthless Rossiter.*

Now Ana was back. Normally, whenever Clarke crossed paths with a girl he'd frequented previously, he never had any difficulty in asserting himself. However, this particular scenario was entirely different, for two significant reasons. Firstly, because in spite of the disappointing manner in which she had chosen to depart so abruptly following their last liaison, coupled with their somewhat terse exchanges today, she still had an effect on him that no other woman had thus far ever managed. Being involved on a personal level was one thing, par for the course even. But when any chosen démoiselle surfaced in the professor's professional life, it was something else entirely. Rossiter couldn't just give Analisse Lejeune the proverbial wide berth in the same way that he sometimes ignored other girls on a purely personal level. Today´s events had tipped the balance completely. The dynamic had changed, and he couldn´t ignore it – or her – any longer.

He would have to resolve this, one way or another. He needed to see her again. Maybe, in spite of himself, he even *wanted* to...

18.

Ana paced around the living room of her modest studio apartment, attempting to process and rationalise the day´s unexpected turn of events. She was an emotional girl at the best of times. But the reappearance of Professor Rossiter had really turned things upside down. They hadn´t been in touch since the last time she´d been with him at his place prior to her precipitated departure, the reasons for which she hadn´t really been able to explain. She had been tempted to call or message him a few times since that last meeting – after all, he´d made such an impression on her – but she had resisted. Seeing him again today in such an alien context had shaken her considerably. As she walked frantically around now, still attempting to come to terms with the day´s events, she was trembling.

She´d arrived home at around six, following a first day of classes that had been – Rossiter revelations notwithstanding – fairly routine. Until *he* had appeared. Yes, Analisse had known that Clarke was a teacher, he´d never attempted to hide the fact. But why oh *why* did he have to pitch up *here* of all places!

Ana wasn't a big drinker – especially not this early in the evening – but the combination of academic stress and the chance meeting with Congletown's master swordsman had caused her to unexpectedly hit the Malibu shortly after arriving home. She set the glass down, flustered and flapping, as she contemplated her next move, worried and irate.

Raising the glass to her lips, she knew that she would have to see him again. If only to sort the situation out and reach some semblance of a conclusion, whether she wanted to or not. As the sweet and sickly pineapple juice mixed with wanton white rum hit the back of her throat, the agitated Ana felt irked not because she had deemed it necessary to see Clarke again and revisit old ground, but because in spite of herself, she actually *wanted* to...

19.

The coffee burned the professor's lips as mug collided abruptly with mouth.

Tossing and turning, patting the pillow down in hopeless bouts of frustrated restlessness...

Rossiter hadn't slept well. The previous day's events had been somewhat testing, and as such, the tumultuous nature of the previous night´s failed attempt at rest was of little surprise to the perplexed and under pressure professor.

At a little after seven, Ana abandoned her fitful efforts to sleep, got up, and headed to the bathroom.

The first few caffeine - fuelled sips did little to rouse Rossiter from his slumber. He was seldom up at such an unusually early hour, wearily shaking his head before meandering to the front door to collect the newspaper from off the mat. He often wondered why he even bothered; the local rag was barely worthy of being called a paper. Congletown, though a pleasant enough place, was hardly home to scandal, or anything remotely shocking, surprising or informative. Only his dearly beloved grandmother ever perused it, if only to consult the obituaries page to see who had succumbed to the grim reaper during the previous week. It was just page after page of the monotonous lives of its inhabitants who, quite frankly, might have resided in just about any normal town anywhere in the country. The professor proceeded to flick through the pages regardless, in a bid to wake himself up before the habitual post – coffee routine of dump, douche and daily grind.

The hot shower did little to relax Ana as she stood under the burning jet, allowing the water to soak her out of her stressed slumber. She was still on edge in the aftermath of the previous day´s events. Even an extremely rare indulgence in alcohol last night had done nothing to quell her anxiety. Stepping out of the shower and grabbing the nearest available towel to envelop her naked body, Analisse knew that she needed to see

Clarke as soon as possible. The situation was already extremely complicated, in light of their having been unexpectedly reacquainted in academic circles. If it were to be allowed to continue, the damage would be potentially irreparable. They had their next class together in three days' time. She resolved to see him before then. There was no other way.

With morning ablutions complete and feeling surprisingly reinvigorated, Clarke took a freshly ironed, crisp navy blue shirt from the wardrobe, and proceeded to prise it from one of the few remaining occupied hangers. *Must do laundry ASAP*, he mused, before towelling off and scouring the underwear drawer which – much like the vast majority of the garments contained therein – had seen better days. New boxers, socks and a chest of drawers – though not the most pant – wettingly exciting of gift ideas – would be top of this year's Christmas list. He could always rely on his mum for love, support... and socks. Tossing his now redundant towel to the bedroom floor, Rossiter lifted his right leg to put on his boxers, almost falling as he did so.

Miss Lejeune firmly closed the front door behind her and proceeded to stride intently though somewhat anxiously down the road, still mulling over the situation in her preoccupied mind. It was nearing eight fifteen as she reached the end of the main boulevard on the edge of town, before finally turning into Newbury Court, propelled by an uncharacteristically strong gust of wind to push her in the direction of where she knew she needed to be...

Still in nothing but his underwear, Clarke disinterestedly ran a comb through his damp hair, barely managing to suppress a grimace as he looked in the mirror at his drawn, almost beleaguered looking face.

As he reached down to pick up a stray sock, once again contemplating the shirt on the bed, the professor was surprised to hear a knock on the front door which grew gradually louder, developing into a full – fisted bang as he irritably made his way through the hall to meet the as yet unknown visitor.

Increasingly flustered and nervous, Ana hurriedly made a beeline for the front door of 14 Newbury Court, almost tripping over a stray pebble as she finally reached her destination. Having knocked for a few seconds to no avail, and becoming evermore frustrated, her light knocking turned to loud hammering as she sought entry into that most familiar of abodes. Growing tired of waiting, she was about to knock again when the key turned in the lock and the door opened, with Rossiter appearing in just his boxers, with damp hair and a look on his face that could best be described as a mixture of surprise and mild irritation.

What the hell is *she* doing here, Clarke thought to himself as he pulled the door back to see Analisse standing before him. But before he´d even had time to collect his thoughts, a petite yet surprisingly strong right hand forced the door open, sending it crashing back against the wall in a crescendo of noise and almost sending the stunned professor sprawling, before he managed to adjust his bare feet and place a hand against the wall to steady himself. The French firecracker darted past him into the hallway:

"What the … Ana?!"

"Well, well! Here we are again, professor! You again! It seems like everywhere I turn, everything I do, you´re there! Bars, social events, and now even at my fucking university, for Christ's sake! You, you, you... it's always *you!* You're *everywhere*! It's too much!"

"Ana..."

"Shut up and let me speak! You're suffocating me! I feel like I can't fucking breathe..."

"And yet *you're* the one who just barged into my house at heaven knows what ungodly hour of the morning, shouting the odds and throwing hissy fits! It's all *very* French of you! You've got the famed Gallic amateur dramatics down to a fine art, if I may say so..."

"No, you may *not* say so... you pompous, arrogant son of a bitch!" Ana's fury was unrelenting, her face incandescent with rage. She was white hot, and Rossiter was rock hard...

Undoubtedly amused but now also slightly agitated, Clarke walked slowly over to Analisse. But in attempting to gently take her hand and motion her to sit down, she erupted again:

"No I will not sit down! This situation is just so messed up! Why does everything always have to be so complicated? I've been awake half the night trying to decide whether I should come to see you, working out exactly what I should say. And then when I arrive, despite the fact that you can clearly see how stressed and confused all this is making me, the most you can muster is a wink and a cocky smirk! You're unbelievable!"

"I know. But thanks anyway. God, you're sexy when you're angry..." he replied, trademark wink and smirk returning no sooner had the words of amused provocation left his lips.

This final quip was too much for Ana to take, one step too far, the proverbial red rag to a bull. She raised the roof again, screaming almost to a wail as she charged across the hallway with both petite French fists clenched, ready to unleash her reignited fury upon the professor. Still shrieking, Ana hammered on Rossiter´s bare chest, before finally looking back up at him, her eyes now moist with tears. It was a look that combined stress, frustration, anger, even a hint of sadness and regret. Clarke grabbed both of Ana´s wrists in an attempt to stop her hitting him. Firmly and authoritatively, but while also remaining calm and ensuring that he didn´t hurt her, Rossiter turned Analisse around and manoeuvred her into the bedroom. He surmised that miss Lejeune wasn´t genuinely angry with him, just confused and frustrated. There was only one way to get rid of all that aggression:

Drop your pants and let´s do the sticky dicky dance...

      Having guided Analisse through the bedroom door, Clarke pushed her against the adjacent wall. He did this firmly and even forcefully, but with no violence or aggression. A playful push and a delicious sound as that most delightful of derrières hit the wall, with Rossiter ruthlessly ripping open the gallic Goddess´ shirt buttons before proceeding to unfasten her short skirt, tossing both garments onto the floor with reckless abandon, revealing navy underwear.

Everything had happened so fast that Ana had hardly even had time to process what was going on, never mind react. Up until just a few short seconds ago, the distressed démoiselle had been a bubbling volcano of pent up anger and frustration. But now, as the professor spun her around to face him, with the still unmade bed behind her, she suddenly felt different... vulnerable. Why?

Because she realised that she wanted him... again.

Another push and she fell backwards onto the bed. Toppling in an act of sexual surrender onto the satin sheets where Rossiter made the magic happen with scores of beautiful women. Ana was still somewhat distressed and perturbed by the realisation that she *wanted* to be there, and that maybe – in spite of herself – that had been why she'd made such a concerted effort to drag her angry self to the (un)safe haven of 14 Newbury Court on this fraught September morning.

She was beginning to comprehend that that morning's situation was entirely different to the first time they'd made sweet amour. On that first occasion, Rossiter had been gentle with Ana, tantalisingly caressing and subsequently devouring her with total self-assurance, but also a distinct and unmistakable tenderness. Today was different, as Clarke now unclipped Ana's bra and tossed it aside, before reaching down to tear off her matching undergarments in a manner that, while not malicious or dangerous, hinted at this ordinarily cool customer appearing to have lost his habitual sense of self – control.

As the second dark blue undergarment was vigorously wrestled from Miss Lejeune's luscious loins and discarded into the corner of the bedroom, which was now pulsing with sexual tension, both performers of the world's favourite and most famous dance realised that the tenderness of their previous encounters had given way to a new type of lovemaking which promised to be harder, faster, more frenetic, and exciting on a whole different level. As rock hard Rossiter slid in and ravaged Ana from behind, pulling her long dishevelled mess of beautiful brown hair as he pounded away, they both knew that they had wanted and *needed* this, a release of their aggression, frustration and confusion in a sweaty mess of tangled torsos and sprawling limbs.

If their first time had been beautiful, elegant, and tender like a waltz or a pasa doble, this morning's particular dance, with its inherent sense of speed, risk and just a hint of provocation and danger, owed more to something resembling a student – teacher tango. Rossiter was calling the tune, and Analisse would have to learn the steps quickly if she were to follow his lead.

    The whole act only lasted a matter of minutes, owing to how horny they both were, and the fast and furious nature of this latest bout of knee – knocking. As they climaxed together and Clarke pulled out, he surprised Ana once again by kissing her softly on the forehead. It was a kiss so gentle – unexpectedly so, given the ferocious nature of their frenzied fornication mere moments earlier – and she was once again blown away by him. As they both lay perspiring and panting breathlessly on the sweat soaked satin, Rossiter firmly tapped Ana on the bottom and motioned for her to get up.

"Come on, clothes on, missy! We need to be getting to class", said the professor, before duly tossing Miss Lejeune her clothes – her new shirt missing not one but two buttons as Rossiter had ripped it from that most beautiful of bodies – and gestured for her to get dressed. Clarke in turn took a navy suit and shirt from off the dressing table – the shirt he'd been preparing to put on before Analisse's unexpected arrival, subsequent aggressive shouting and what had followed – and began to dress hurriedly.

They arrived a few minutes later than normal at the university, given the morning's wholly unexpected turn of events, making sure not to be seen together as they neared Congletown's revered white gates. Approaching the entrance, they made sure to go their separate ways as inconspicuously as possible, with Ana looking flustered and giving an almost apologetic wave, countered by a self-satisfied, almost smug smirk from Rossiter as he strode belatedly but relaxedly to his office. The first class – for which he was almost ten minutes late – was with a group of postgraduate students, of which there were only four. Usually only three turned up as one particular student rarely bothered to attend, doubtless due to one of the many problems that seemingly blighted today's youth.

Analisse had no classes from nine until twelve that morning, so she decided to go to the Edmund Royle library to do some pre-seminar reading. However hard she endeavoured to study, though, her mind always came back to the professor. He and this whole absurd situation was becoming almost an addiction for her. She knew that it couldn't continue as such, and that them continuing to be anything other than teacher and student was utterly inconceivable. But she was drawn to him – and doubtless he to her. As Ana attempted to delve into the books in a bid to maintain at least *some* degree of concentration, all that she was able to focus on was Clarke's dick inside her – and how fucking *good* it felt.

Rossiter's day went pretty much as expected. The postgrads were entertaining as usual, and then he had to endure two afternoon classes with Congletown's first and second years, sandwiched between more bullshit administrative tasks in the staff room and a hastily taken coffee break. So, when he lumbered through the door at around six in the evening, slouching onto the sofa, the first thing he thought about was a nice cold beer, which he duly went to get from the fridge. He sipped contentedly on the amber nectar, and realised that he hadn't even thought about Ana all day, as he hadn't had time to. Despite her fury upon arriving at his house that morning, the sex had been great as ever, and he was looking forward to seeing her again. However, as he got up off the sofa and went out onto the bandstand, he knew that he wouldn't have cause to think about Analisse Lejeune again. He was off to the Playhouse tonight, and there could be no room for distractions.

20.

Swinging those oh so familiar doors open and striding the short distance to the bar, Clarke was happy to be back at the Playhouse – back home. Sidling towards the bar and winking at his old friend Beni Rothwell as she went off to get a beer for another thirsty customer, Rossiter found an unoccupied barstool and made himself comfortable, seeing beautiful but inexperienced barmaid Carla from the corner of his eye, and duly motioning her over.

"Carla! Great to see you! It's been a while! How's my favourite accountancy student this evening? I hope Spain hasn't stolen mine and everyone else's hard - earned money!"

"Claaaarrrrke!"

It was almost a screech, as she returned from checking a text message, throwing her phone away and re - emerging from the back of the bar to greet the professor. The look on her face was one of playfulness as always, with dancing eyes and a wondrous smile, a truly phenomenal body enveloped in a tight black top and jeans. Carla Valencia was brown eyes, beautiful boobs, a knowingly sassy wink and, as the terrible music kicked in, dire dance moves befitting a lass her age. Being twenty – three will do that to a girl.

With brash booty shaking over and boobies no longer bouncing, Clarke ordered a beer and took a swig as soon as it landed on the mahogany in front of him, winking at Carla in the process. She was in her second year studying to be an accountant at a private school in one of the nearby towns. Although Rossiter was always very vigilant with regard to his financial matters, and would never entrust a woman to look after or spend his money, Carla Valencia was the one girl he *might* make an exception for. She was absolutely stunning, quite definitely the most jaw – droppingly beautiful woman he had ever met... with the exception of Analisse Lejeune, of course. Carla's surname was also that of her home city. Born and raised in Valencia, Spain's third largest (and undoubtedly best) city, Carla had started working at the Playhouse to help pay for her studies. And though it were true that (almost) all the barmaids there were attractive, Carla the Costa Blanca cutie was without doubt the star attraction. Rossiter jokingly called her his *Spanish wife*, and teased that he would marry her one day. Here she was tonight, absolutely *smokin'* hot... and he wanted her.

As spectacular as Carla was, however, the professor had other things – and indeed other people – on his mind tonight. He took a fleeting glance at his watch and saw that it was just after nine. Tonight one of his dearest friends – who went by the delightful name of Stan Pleasures – was flying in from France for a long overdue visit. Rossiter and Stan had first met many years previously, in the French town where they'd both lived, and where Pleasures still resided. When they'd first met all those years ago in France's sun dappled deep south, Stan had been plying his trade as an ice cream vendor, almost single handedly managing and running the shop due to his boss frequently taking lengthy breaks, holidays and such. Several years of serving scoops had eventually begun to take its toll on young Mr. Pleasures, however. So in the midst of yet another sweltering summer of strawberry swirls and sexy girls, he'd decided to abandon ice cream and ice queens, embarking on a new career as a cocktail mixologist in his newly opened bar – Pleasures and Double Measures.

Clarke swigged his beer, trying his hardest to keep his eyes off Carla, and cast a glance along the bar towards the other side of the room. One of the intriguing things about the Playhouse was that it had not one, but two main rooms. The first one, right by the entrance, was very much a bar area with a relaxed, chilled out vibe. The second room – separated by the famous red curtain – was more like a nightclub. Rossiter spent time in both rooms, primarily due to the fact that the barmaids often alternated between working the two main bars, Carla included. The professor preferred the more relaxed bar area, by virtue of the fact that it was quieter, and always the first port of call for the ample array of hot girls that stopped to order a drink upon entering the venue.

With eyes fixed on the red curtain, there didn't seem to be much going on as yet. Clarke took another sip of beer and raised his glass to one of the other barmen he knew. He knew them all, not just the barmaids. The guys working there were pretty cool too, actually. He was always greeted warmly by everybody there, from the security guys on the door to all of the bar staff. Rossiter was on first name terms with all of the Playhouse posse, and one of them always brought him a barstool as soon as he came in.

VIP, baby.

As he shifted on his seat again in an attempt to adjust and find a more comfortable sitting position, Clarke felt a tap on his left shoulder, and duly swivelled around. Standing before him with a beaming smile on his face was his boy, Stan Pleasures.

"Hello you!"

"Mr. Pleasures, it's been *far* too long!"

"Yes it has. But enough of the small talk, I want beer and girls! Now! Where are our Spanish wives?"

"The dream team are both working tonight! Carla and Hannah are both here!", replied Rossiter, referring to both of his and Stan's favourite Playhouse hotties. Pleasures had immediately taken a shine to Hannah when he'd first visited. As a consequence, both he and Clarke had nicknamed the Playhouse's perfect pair their *Spanish wives.*

No sooner had he mentioned their names than Hannah strutted over.

"Hannah! Another beer for my man, please! You remember Stan, right?"

"Sure! Hello Stan!" she said with a teasing smirk. "It´s been a while. How have you been?"

"Hello wife! I´m very well, thanks. All the better for seeing you!" Hannah tutted, playfully shoved Stan´s arm and then winked before sidling off to serve another customer.

"God, Clarkey boy, I´ve missed this place! And you! So many hot girls here! It´s game time!"

"It´s good to have you back! Let´s get on it!"
They downed their beers, shuffled down from their barstools and headed for the red curtain to scour for lady flower.

They wandered through the steadily increasing crowds, and slipped through the curtain, heading towards the other bar where Carla now happened to be working, presumably having swapped places with Hannah. As Clarke glanced over to his right, he could tell straight away that Stan was surveying the scene for any cute girls. Stan was an absolutely amazing guy, salt of the earth, and like Rossiter, he loved the ladies. It was fair to say that Mister Pleasures had even more success with women than Clarke. He was better looking, and had bags of charisma but wasn´t arrogant with it. Stan was just a genuinely good man, and one of Clarke best friends. *Now it was time to play.*

The professor noticed that Stan was no longer by his side. With eyes darting left and right, it didn´t take him long to work out where his friend had got to. He´d been quick to procure two vacant seats at the bar, and was sitting in anticipation of Clarke's arrival.

"There you are! I'd wondered how long it'd take before you got thirsty again..."

He motioned Carla over.

"Carla, you remember Stan? He's back!"

"Hola guapo! Muy buenas! Una beer?" she enquired, giggling.

"Errrr.... yes, por favor!"

As Carla went off in search of the ice cream dream team's latest liquid refreshment, Stan looked across at Clarke and smirked.

"Wow! Your wife is hot! Spanish girls are great!"

"That they are! Even better after a few beers! Get that down you!"

Carla had put two icy cold beers down in front of them, accompanied by her now customary wink.

"Cheers, Stanley! I propose a toast, to beer and rear!"

"To beer and beautiful Spanish rear!"

As they sat and sipped, Stan and Clarke talked about the usual things: football, girls, family, work, with Rossiter's friend excitedly announcing that Pleasures and Double Measures was proving to be a real success, despite only having opened its doors the previous month. Stan – unsurprisingly – had employed half a dozen stunningly beautiful barmaids to serve cocktails for him. Producing his phone from his pocket, Stan proceeded to show Clarke photos of each of the new ravishing recruits, chuckling as he did so.

"They're all fucking *ridiculously* hot! They're gonna make cocktails for me, and I'm hopefully gonna be putting my cock in them. Supply and demand, one of the first considerations of good business!"

"Amen to that... and to *that*!", replied Clarke, nudging Stan to draw his attention to the fact that the two previously unoccupied barstools immediately to their right had been taken by a couple of absolute babes. Pleasures put the phone back into his pocket, and with a self assured smile, nodded to Rossiter to acknowledge that now, at long last, it was time to play the game, and both star players were in the house.
Pleasures and Rossiter: the Dream Team.

Stan raised his glass in the direction of the two new arrivals, holding out his right hand with a smirk:

"Alright girls! I´m Stan and this is Clarke. You two look lovely!"

"Hi! I´m Danielle, and this is Roberta. Don´t be fooled... I´m the shy one..."

Stan chuckled and shifted over to become better acquainted with Danielle, giving the green light for Clarke to move closer to Roberta, offering a warm smile as he introduced himself:

"Roberta, huh? A quite glorious name for a dazzling dame! That smile tells me *you´re* not shy. Am I right?"

"Dead right!"

"Haha, confident *and* cute! What *am* I going to do with you?"

"Well, you can start by getting me another one of those", she replied, gesturing towards an almost empty gin and tonic on the bar.

They talked some more, with Rossiter and Stan both getting their respective girl´s number and promising to come back and find them before the night was out, after more drinks. They were both now becoming steadily more inebriated – or ruined, as Pleasures often called it - and, slinking off their barstools, set off in search of new girls. Both men were remarkably similar where their attitudes to women were concerned. Despite having considerable success with the ladies – more so than Clarke – Stan´s mentality had changed somewhat in recent times, as a consequence of having, upon occasion, fallen for the wrong types of girls who had subsequently hurt him emotionally. But now, despite a few difficult times in the not too distant past, Stan was back to his best. He´d decided that he didn´t want the drama that so many women seemed to bring to the table; Clarke could certainly relate to that. What they needed after so much time apart was some man time, beers and laughs. Women could wait... for now.

    Just as they were deliberating over what to drink next and where, Stanley spotted Hannah out of the corner of his roving eye. He smirked and strode intently over to the bar:

  "Hannah, tell me, do you like challenges?"

  "Haha! Depend of the challenge, I guess. Sorry, I no speak English very good."

  "Ok, well, I want you to make me a cocktail of your choosing. You can make whatever you like. But there is a rule: you may only use a maximum of five ingredients. Cinco ingredientes! Ok?"

  "And what if I don´t like to obey the rules, mister English man?" she answered with a flirtatious, teasing wink.

  "Even better", Stan replied, chuckling and high fiving her in the process. He turned to his buddy with a beaming smile as Hannah turned away to begin making his surprise cocktail.

"I think I love her! She is *almost* perfect. And she'll look even better as I get more ruined! She likes cocktails. I bet she likes cock, too!"

"Haha, oh mate I've missed you!" Rossiter gestured to Carla, who had now returned from the other bar, and requested two more beers, surmising that they'd still have ample time to drink them while they waited for Hannah to finish Stan's mystery concoction.

As Carla plonked the beers down before them – having once again taken to dancing badly as she did so – they swigged contentedly as the cerveza coated their thirsty throats in hoppy heaven.

"Oh god, that's good! Although I must say I'm drinking less beer these days. The cocktail thing is great fun. I'm so happy I made the change!"

Stan went on to explain to Clarke how he'd decided to leave his ice cream days behind and embark upon this new venture into cocktaildom. He'd started with a month of training in the "big smoke", making magic mixtures and wowing women with nightly displays of showman like bottle twirling, before deciding to take the plunge and open Pleasures & Double Measures upon his return home. As he recounted to Rossiter a series of stories and anecdotes about his new venture, it became quite clear that Stan was made to be a mixer, a master of Mojitos. Clarke was delighted for his friend. He'd had a tough time and deserved a break. Stan Pleasures was well and truly on the up.

Having detailed his plans for the new bar, Stan scanned the Playhouse again for new girls he liked the look of. As he did so, he heard a light thud as Hannah placed the cocktail – which Stan had decided to christen 'Pleasure in a Glass' - atop the bar.

"Try my new creation, crazy English man!" she said with a smile which subsequently broke into a laugh.

"I´m only crazy when Spanish girls are around! They – and especially *you* – are a bad influence on me! I´m a good boy, most of the time..."

"Haha! Taste the drink, tell me if you like or no!" retorted Hannah, her expectant brown eyes melting like dark chocolate as she looked at him in anticipation.

"Well Hannah, just so you know, if I like your drink I´m taking you home with me tonight...", said Stan with a smirk and a wink as he raised the dark purple, plum coloured concoction to his lips. Pleasures proceeded to swirl the new beverage around his mouth, before swallowing and turning to Hannah, who was still eagerly looking on.

"Well Hannah, do you want the good news or the bad news?"

"Errr... the bad? I don´t know..." she said, leaning slightly nervously across the bar with a flustered, mildly agitated expression on her almost angelic visage.

"Well... the bad news is that your attempt at a cocktail tastes absolutely awful!"

Hannah glared back at Stan, sullen, disappointed, almost shocked at her apparent failure to tickle his taste buds.

"Annn... annnd the good?", she stuttered in response, with arms now folded, almost in an act of defiance.

Seeing how irked Hannah had become merely served to amuse Stan further.

"The good news, Hannah, is that I´m only joking! I *did* like your drink, and it´s cute that you made such an effort for me. You´re more than just a pretty face, after all. So I´m going to take you home tonight, and we can practise making drinks together! Didn´t I tell you that I´m a cocktail expert myself? I will teach you some tricks of the trade. But only if you promise to be a *good* girl..."

Stan flashed another grin her way and winked suggestively, almost provocatively at her. Hannah smirked back at him and hit him playfully on the arm across the bar. It was clear that any annoyance she´d shown seconds earlier had disappeared, and that her new, disgruntled expression was clearly feigned, and purely for show.

"Qué malo eres, mister Englishman! You are bad person! I no sé if I go in your house..."

The smattering of Spanglish in Hannah´s sexy accent caused Stan to burst out laughing, projecting a beaming smile in her direction as she turned away to serve another customer, winking at him as she did so.

It was game on.

Having finished the cocktail and subsequently a couple more beers apiece, Rossiter and Pleasures decided that it was time to leave. As Clarke took his jacket from his chair and slid it around his broad shoulders, he looked around. Stan had disappeared from by his side, and as the professor scanned the surroundings, he noticed that his friend had walked around to the other side of the bar, handed Hannah his jacket, and was proceeding to guide her out from behind the mahogany, with his right hand across her lower back in a showing of clear intent as he guided her out of the

Playhouse door. Hannah, smiling and undoubtedly impressed at Stan's display of confidence, called over her shoulder to a smirking Carla, asking her to fill in for her, given that it was now only a few short minutes to closing time. Rossiter followed them outside with an amused shake of the head as they went in search of a taxi, waving at a now chuckling Carla as he vacated the premises.

They didn't have to wait long for a ride home. After only a couple of minutes, Clarke's friend Vincent rolled around the corner in his pristine white cab, tooting at him with a delighted wave. He pulled up outside, opening the doors to allow Clarke, Stan and Hannah to climb in.

"El profesor! How are you?" enquired Vincent, clearly happy to see his friend.

"Molt be, gràcies amic!" replied Rossiter in Valencian. He only knew a few words in Vincent's native tongue, but he occasionally used it when talking to certain friends who hailed from those parts. The language of Spain's third city – which Rossiter had visited following his time in France, and would doubtless go back to someday – was a mixture of French and Spanish, both of which Rossiter spoke, along with reasonable German and basic Italian.

He'd always loved foreign languages, ever since he'd started learning français under the tutelage of Lil Prickles, his first ever teacher of foreign lingo. She'd been a big influence on Rossiter's academic background when he'd started secondary school, along with English teacher Troy Fewings, and Nat McDonald, who'd been another of Clarke's teachers beforehand, during his final year at primary school. Having quickly discovered his flair for writing, she'd been the first to actively encourage the young Clarke to pursue it as a career. It was fair to say that those three esteemed members of Congletown's educational hierarchy had had a significant and lasting influence on Rossiter's opting for a career in the written word and foreign languages.

    The professor's early steps into academia seemed a lifetime ago now, however, as the taxi glided around Congletown's street corners towards number 14 Newbury Court, the darkness of the mild night punctuated by a yawning yellow light from the glow of street lamps lining the roads, as Vincent's car moved towards its destination. Looking in the mirror, Clarke could see that Stan and Hannah were smiling at one another in seductive expectation, with his right hand gently caressing his favourite Spanish señorita's denim clad, shapely left thigh as the cab pulled into Rossiter's driveway.

    As they piled out of the taxi and Clarke bid Vincent goodnight, he was all too aware that Stan was already at the front door, with his hand placed intently upon Hannah's pert, peachy backside, giving it a playful slap as Rossiter unlocked the door and motioned them inside. As he tossed his jacket aside and headed into the kitchen to make drinks and noting Stan and Hannah's flirting, Rossiter began to rue the fact that Carla had been unable to join them that evening. She had a boyfriend, but Clarke hoped that it wouldn't last, and that he might be able to make inroads with her in the not too distant future. Apart from Analisse Lejeune, Carla Valencia was – quite literally – the most beautiful woman he had *ever* known. In fact, she was probably more beautiful than Ana, physically speaking. But

Analisse seemed to have some kind of *hold* over him that no other woman had ever come close to. He now thought about Ana every single day, and the fact that she had unexpectedly become his student would do little to help the situation.

Taking three glasses from the cupboard and duly setting them upon the sideboard, Rossiter left the kitchen and ventured into the lounge to ask Stan and Hannah what they both wanted to drink. He guessed beer for Pleasures and red wine for the Spanish siren and, predictions being correct, walked straight back to serve their chosen beverages.

"Here you are, Hannah. This is a lovely Spanish number, cheeky and robust, like your good self. I wasn't sure whether you'd be a Rioja or a Ribera del Duero kind of girl, so it's a good job I've got vast quantities of both. Here's a Rioja to start with."

She willingly accepted the glass and began sipping, tentatively at first, before allowing a little more of the ruby red liquid to slip into that most majestic of mouths, savouring the flavour before setting her glass aside and sliding along the sofa to be nearer to Stan, who duly took her hand and gave her a kiss; a quick peck, a light, lingering touch on those most luscious of lips. The cock – tease from Córdoba nuzzled her head against Stan's shoulder, clearly at home in the welcoming warmth of Rossiter's living room.

"It's a real pity Carla couldn't be here with us tonight", interjected Clarke, still slightly frustrated that his preferred Playhouse pint puller hadn't been able to join them. He'd just have to hope that he'd be able to bring her back to his place soon. He fancied his chances, given the way that she continually flirted with him. But Rossiter wanted to get to know her better, in a different venue and context to that of the bar. So far, all he really knew about her was that she was Spanish, that she studied accountancy, and that she was hot. He wanted – and needed – to get Analisse Lejeune out of his head. Carla Valencia was the *perfect* way to do so. She and Hannah España were both colleagues and friends; if Rossiter played his cards right, he could use Hannah to bring Carla closer to him.

"Yeah, but she work a lot, you know. She no really have mucho time, with study and feina. But I think she like you. She tell me muchas veces, Clarke..."

"Is that so?"

"Yes. I think maybe she love you. Enamorada... hihi."

This was the best possible music to Rossiter´s ears. He would have to bring out his ´A´ game again next time he saw her.

The three of them sat and continued drinking for about another hour, before Stan gently picked Hannah up off the sofa, and winking at Clarke, guided his *Spanish wife* to the bedroom, kissing her as he led her away. It was clear that Hannah would be getting pleasured tonight.

Clarke too finished a final glass of wine, tidied up the living room to what he considered to be an acceptable level (whatever *that* meant), and turned in. He tossed and turned for a few minutes, but couldn´t sleep because of the increasing noise coming from the guest room down the corridor. It appeared little miss Córdoba was getting quite the VIP treatment.

Well played, Stanley.

21.

Rossiter rose early the next morning, and wandered sluggishly into the kitchen to make coffee. There being no sign of Stan or Hannah, he surmised that they must still be in bed; they ought to be tired, given that the screaming Spaniard had kept him awake until nearly 4 am. Stan had obviously been worthy of his surname, and a man deserved his rest.

Stretching as the coffee brewed, Clarke looked out of the kitchen window and noticed Lexi the Peruvian neighbour having her customary morning swim. The professor had seen very little of her since they'd last had drinks together; with the academic year at Congletown gathering pace, he hadn't had time to suggest that they reacquaint themselves, and hadn't been inclined to make the effort. She was hot, but she'd come to him if she wanted to. Clarke never made much effort with any particular woman, as it wasn't necessary, and often proved to be a waste of time.

As he sat sipping the nation's favourite caffeine fuelled hot beverage and stifling a yawn, Rossiter's mind went back to the events of the previous night. He and Stan had had great fun, as was always the case. It'd been too long since they'd seen one another – almost three years - and Clarke decided that he would make an effort to see his friend more often, whether that be at his place or Stan's.

It was now just after 10 am – still relatively early in Rossiter terms – and the professor felt decidedly jaded. His sleep had been fitful at best, which wasn´t surprising given the fun that Stan and Hannah had appeared to be having in the guest room until the early hours. He would be sure to quiz his friend about it when he surfaced later. The coffee was thus far failing to have much of an effect and, still feeling groggy, Clarke made a second cup and walked into the living room, before sitting sleepily down upon the sofa and turning on the television. It was the usual Saturday morning fare; namely kids´ cartoons, sports news, and cookery programmes. Clarke wasn´t much of a chef, but he did enjoy his occasional culinary experiments. He had a few favourite dishes that he knew how to make reasonably well, and although his repertoire was far from extensive, various women had praised his efforts whenever he´d cooked for them in the past.

Having finished a second cup of coffee, watched some sports news and read his beloved football team´s online forum for a few minutes thereafter – that of Fort Dale – Clarke was just about to lie down on the couch when Stan entered the room, unleashing a rasping fart and subsequently bursting out laughing as he did so.

"It lives! It farts!"

"Haha! Yeah, baby!"

"Sounded like you and little miss Córdoba had fun last night!"

"God, she´s hot! A crackerjack in the sack! Fun too! I really like her..."

"Good man. Is she still asleep after last night´s exertions?"

"Yeah. I wanted to stay with her, but my arse stinks! I need a dump before I can even think about entertaining her again..." replied Stan, and with that, he beat a hasty retreat to the bathroom, smirking at Rossiter and farting again as he left the room.

Rossiter, almost gagging at the putrid odour, turned over on the sofa in the hope of being able to nap for a while longer. After tossing and turning, however, he gave up and went to make breakfast. After forcing down two slices of toast to battle the hangover, which proved to be quite an ordeal, he went for a shower to try and blow away the cobwebs. Easier said than done after a night out with Mister Stanley Pleasures. Experience had taught him that, long ago.

    Feeling slightly better having showered, the professor mused over what to do today. He wasn´t much for class preparation, and what little he *did* do was always left until Sunday. Saturday was not a day for academic toil. He and Stan would doubtless go and have a lunch of the liquid variety, then relax in the afternoon before yet another night out. Girls and booze were what made these two young men´s lives more fun and entertaining. They were both in their thirties, and despite what anybody said of the partners in crime, they both led fantastic lives, and enjoyed them to the full. This long – awaited weekend of Pleasures promised to ensure that the debauchery would continue.

    After having taken what seemed like an eternity, Stanley emerged from the bathroom, hurriedly closing the door behind him.

"Oooof! That fuckin´ stinks! Haha! I wouldn´t go in there for a while if I were you! God, I hope sleeping beauty doesn´t need to use the facilities anytime soon!"

"Haha! You´re an animal!" retorted Clarke, before picking up a cup of coffee from off the nearby table and handing it to his friend. "What are our plans today? I thought a bite to eat and some afternoon liquid refreshment, then a nap before we head out again tonight. Thoughts?"

"Sounds like a plan, Clarkey boy! I need to bid farewell to little miss Córdoba first, though..."

"Yeah, no problem. We´re not in any hurry anyway."

Stan went back to the bedroom – presumably to wake Hannah – as a few short minutes later, giggling, moaning and the creaking of the spare room bed were all audible as Rossiter turned up the TV volume in an attempt to block out the sound of his buddy and the sexy Spaniard enjoying round two. The pair of them emerged about forty – five minutes later, with Hannah walking behind Stan, her arms around his waist and her head of dishevelled dark hair posed upon his muscly brown back.

"Well well well... good morning you two", chirped Clarke as the new lovebirds sat sleepily down on the sofa.

"Morniiiing Clarrrrke!" replied Hannah with a tired drawl.

"Sounds like you two had fun back there!"

"Haha, yes! It was quite the wake up call your buddy just gave me!" Hannah answered, complete with a contented smile as she looked dreamily over at Stan.

"What are your plans today?"

"I need coffee – naughty niño Stanley sapped all my energy! But then I need to go. I have some things to do at home before I go and see my family. But I will call you later, mister Pleasure man, to make sure you´re not being a naughty boy while I´m gone", teased the Spanish siren, nuzzling Stan´s neck and giving him a kiss before heading into the kitchen to make coffee.

"Ok, baby. Have a coffee, then get your sexy little self showered, and I will talk to you tonight. Clarke and I have a busy day ahead of us!" replied Stan with a customary smirk and trademark wink.

Hannah made and drank a quick coffee, got showered and dressed then left, kissing and hugging Stan and waving goodbye to Rossiter as she slinked out of the door, beseeching her new beau to call her later.

"So, Stanley... will you call her? Or are you gonna keep her guessing?" enquired a curious Clarke.

"Oh, I´ll definitely call her. But I´ll take my time, keep her on her toes for a bit. Any girl loves a bit of mystery and nervous tension. But I´d be a fool not to contact her, especially after a night like that! She´s absolutely fucking glorious, I tell you!"

"Right you are!"

The two young lotharios proceeded to don presentable attire, before heading out for an inebriated afternoon which was much more liquid than luncheon. The rest of Stan´s Congletown visit followed much the same pattern; namely laughs, lager and ladies. He made sure to catch up again with Hannah before he left, promising to stay in touch and jokingly referring to her as one of his many *girls in every port*. Whether or not he´d keep such a promise, only time would tell. Following a hungover attempt at breakfast on the final day of this most salacious of sunny sojourns, Rossiter accompanied Stan to the airport to bid him a fond farewell.

"So long, buddy. I´m gonna fucking miss you like a nympho misses nipples!"

"Haha! Oh, Mr. Rossiter... any more of this loin-dampening love speak, and you might just force me to stay!"

"As delightful as that would doubtless be, you, my good sir, have a new bar to run, Mojitos to mix and barmaids to bang. As much as it pains me to say it, and shrouds me in chagrin, you have a plane to catch! Be gone with you!"

Hence, they emotionally embraced; the mother of all man hugs, with Rossiter promising to visit Stan as soon as work would allow him to do so. He was eager to run the rule over Pleasures & Double Measures, and swore not to leave it so long before returning to see his pal on those fabled Provençal shores of which he'd grown so fond.

Stan strode away, glancing back with a wave and a grin as he approached the boarding gate. Clarke chuckled as his friend made his way to catch his impending flight, safe in the knowledge that they'd see each other soon.

With farewells complete, the professor left the airport and made his way back to Congletown, a journey of around forty minutes along leafy country lanes back to his home town. Whilst Congletown wasn't a particularly exciting or vibrant place, it was safe, cosy, and a perfect environment for anyone wishing to start and raise a young family. Rossiter had lived in places other than his home town, and had had numerous happy experiences in all of them. But despite his many years living abroad, Congletown would always be *home*.

As he arrived home, reflecting upon what a wonderful time he'd had with Stan, an unexpected sight struck him as he walked tiredly down the drive.

Who should be standing at his front door other than Analisse Lejeune....
Fatigued and still mildly hungover after his weekend of over indulgence in the demon drink with Stan, unexpectedly setting eyes upon Ana threatened to send Clarke into something of a tailspin. For although seeing the Frenchy was always a pleasure for Rossiter – physically speaking at least – he wasn't sure he had the energy for what would doubtless be yet another emotionally charged altercation with his favourite voluptuous vixen. Not again... not now.

Upon reaching the front door of number fourteen, the professor attempted to regain a measure of composure, before acknowledging her presence:

"Analisse. You're the last person I expected to see here. What brings you back? I've had a heavy weekend. Aggro is the last thing on my mind right now..."

She looked back at him, diminutive frame swaying perhaps slightly nervously as their eyes met. There she was, hands on hips and loitering with intent. Her body language and determined demeanour indicated that she meant business.

"Hello Clarke."

"What are you doing here?"

Ana shifted her feet uneasily, as she attempted to keep her balance as he fixed his tired brown eyes upon her.

"Let's go inside. We need to talk."

"Madre mía! Those are words no sane man ever wants to hear..."

Ana's quick tilt of the head to the side, coupled with a tut, served to further highlight her impatience and an all too apparent wish to get everything off that all too inviting chest of hers.

Clarke fought off a lingering feeling of lethargy to prise the front door key from his pocket. As the door opened with a creak and he invited Analisse over the threshold and duly followed, it was becoming all too apparent that the irritated stare, coupled with miss Lejeune´s impatient tone of voice – one almost bordering on hostility – hinted that this latest exchange would be unlikely to end well for Mr. Rossiter.

"Drink, little Miss France?" proffered Clarke as he almost instinctively crossed the hall into the kitchen.

"No."

"What? Not even a little snifter, missy?"

"Fuck you, Clarke! I said no! No means NO!"

Despite her tetchiness – unwarranted though it seemed to Clarke – the professor still mustered a smile as he sat down on the sofa, before motioning Analisse over to sit next to him. As she reluctantly did so, Clarke´s overriding impression that the latest chapter in this burgeoning gallic and phallic parable wouldn´t be one for the faint hearted, seemed increasingly likely...

Now both sitting comfortably on Rossiter´s sofa, the Congletown conqueror edged closer to Ana and attempted to kiss her. Her rebuttal surprised him somewhat, as it seemed a perfectly normal and natural thing to do, given the intimacy of their recent encounters. But as Clarke moved in to kiss her again, Ana moved away, leaving him in no doubt as to her unwillingness to indulge in flighty feminine fancies; she wasn´t interested in flirting or foreplay of any description whatsoever, a point hammered home to a disappointed Rossiter with that all too familiar turning of the cheek that he still found so tempting.

Having been unexpectedly rebuffed – it wasn't something that happened to him very often – Rossiter was beginning to lose patience.

"Okay, Ana. You want to talk? I'm waiting.... start talking."
The Paris born English teacher shuffled uneasily as she prepared to unburden herself with whatever revelations were about to come Clarke's way. She seemed hesitant and looked guilty – almost sad – as she turned back to face him before quickly looking down at her feet, her gaze seemingly unwilling – or perhaps unable – to meet the professor's:

"We can't be together, Clarke. This – whatever *this* is or is threatening to turn into – has to stop *now*. Forever. You and me... it's just not possible, I'm afraid."
As Rossiter looked back at her, his expression was one of sadness, shock, and absolute incredulity.

"Not possible... you're afraid?! Well, you didn't seem to be too afraid when I was treating you like a Princess, taking you to fancy restaurants and when you had my dick inside you!", boomed the professor, almost screaming his tirade into the sheepish face of a shell-shocked Analisse.

"What?! What are you saying? You have absolutely *no* right to talk to me that way! I already told you that I didn't want anything complicated. All of this is just too much! It's too complicated, and that's *your* fault, not mine!"

"My fault?! Okay, I get that you might have had doubts about us, about whatever's happened between us so far. But you weren't exactly vocal in

your resistance when things suited you! If you had any misgivings about how things were progressing between us, you should've been much clearer about how you felt. Jesus, Ana!"

"I know that, Clarke, I know..."

"You know what, Ana? The more time I spend with you and the more I listen to you talk, the more I realise that almost *everything* you say or do has an agenda. You were more than happy to be around me when there was something for you to get out of us being in each other's company. But now that the waters appear to have become muddied, you decide to escape confronting your feelings or making any kind of rational decision, and lo and behold, you run for the hills!"

"Clarke..."

"Oh, save it, Ana! I'm sick of your bullshit! I'm right to use that word, on the basis that you haven't even given me a proper reason as to why we supposedly can't be together."

Analisse knew that the time had come for some potentially devastating home truths. As Clarke looked across at her, almost sneering as he prepared his next rebuke, he saw tears welling up in Ana's now desolate blue green eyes. She was good at that – turning on the waterworks whenever things started to go awry – a fact not lost on Rossiter as he indignantly shook his head, impatiently waiting for answers.
A solitary, solemn tear proceeded to roll down Ana's cheek, as she attempted to gather her thoughts. With her eyes and the side of her face still moist, she looked directly at Rossiter, endeavouring to compose herself through the sadness:

"Listen, Clarke. This isn´t easy to say. I can´t be with you, because I can´t be with another disabled guy..."

"What?"

Analisse looked down at the floor, and more tears flowed.

"Whenever I see you – and your disability – it´s almost as though I´m seeing little bits of myself in the mirror. I can´t and won´t do it. Anything that you and I have or had, cannot and will not continue. I like you, Clarke. I would like us to stay friends, or at least stay in touch. But that is up to you..."

Analisse picked up her jacket and bag, and hastily made for the door. Clarke looked left and right, bemusedly attempting to gather his thoughts.

"Wow! So now.... just as things once again start to get difficult for you, Ana, you run? Things get tricky, and little miss Lejeune escapes? I don´t even know why 1´m surprised anymore."

"I´m sorry, Clarke. Really, I am", said Ana as she shuffled across the hallway and out of the door, with a raging Rossiter duly slamming it unceremoniously behind her.

22.

  The next few weeks and months passed fairly uneventfully. Clarke still had classes with Analisse, but they were due to finish soon, and in any case, she hadn´t been to a single one since the situation between them had come to a head. The professor had managed to compartmentalise the personal and the professional in his mind, and draw a line in the sand; as much as it hurt, Analisse Lejeune didn´t want him. He would do everything in his power to get over her, starting with another Playhouse Saturday night in a matter of hours.

  Rossiter always had a few beers with the other teachers after work on a Friday. But he couldn't overdo it, given that he taught a three – hour class every Saturday morning. Said class had gone well that day, as was usually the case, and now after a quick dash to the supermarket, and with the time approaching three o'clock, Clarke settled down with a beer on the bandstand, ready to watch his beloved Fort Dale team play online. They were in action every Saturday afternoon, with the occasional Tuesday night game. Living away from the hallowed Blursem turf, the professor paid a yearly subscription in order to be able to tune in to every single game from elsewhere. It wasn't the same as actually *being* there at his spiritual home, but it was the next best thing. Watching his team was one of the few instances which forced Clarke to concede that modern technology *did* have its merits on occasion, allowing him to watch his beloved black and whites from afar.

      Rossiter still got the same buzz of nervous anticipation every Saturday prior to kick – off. His walks to the supermarket were not only a necessary errand in buying the usual weekly provisions, but they also served as a means of clearing his head before a game. Clarke became a totally different person when football was involved; a completely different animal. Clichéd though it doubtless appeared to outsiders at times, Fort Dale Football Club was so much more than just a team to Rossiter. Following them through thick and thin for the last thirty-odd years had given Clarke so many memorable moments, both of joy and agony. The fact that he'd chosen to support his local team due to them being the closest one to Congletown, and also by virtue of the invaluable footballing education given to him by his stepfather – a former professional player and subsequent employee of the club following retirement – meant so much. Fort Dale weren't, had never been and probably never would be, particularly famous or successful. But the fact that they were the underdog – as Rossiter himself had been on so many occasions – suited the professor. In fact, he revelled in it. Much like Dale, existing in the shadow of the other team nearby, the name of which Rossiter refused to utter, Clarke had never had things easy. He had had to struggle for absolutely everything that he'd achieved throughout his life. So the idea of being the underdog and having to fight for success in the face of adversity was something that he could easily relate to. For this reason, Clarke Rossiter and Fort Dale Football Club were the perfect match; not just a team that played on Saturday afternoons, but a way of life that bordered on obsession, or even addiction.

    The professor had attended hundreds of games over the years, spoken on local radio about the team, and even acted as a voluntary interpreter for two French - speaking players a few years previously; it had been the happiest and proudest day of his entire life. As a young man, Rossiter had even invested some of his own money in order to save his beloved club along with a thousand or so other supporters, when the Dale had fallen on particularly hard times financially. Hence, he'd become a shareholder. Although Clarke enjoyed teaching, it wasn't his true passion. That label belonged – and would only *ever* belong – to Fort Dale Football Club. His dream job, unrealistic though it perhaps was, had always been to manage his team. As a younger man, he'd often despaired of the fact that his physical disability would never allow him to take up a role that he viewed not only as the most important in football, but one which – to this young man at least – was the greatest job in the *entire* world. It had taken him a long time to accept the fact that he would never have the opportunity to occupy that hottest of hot seats, even though he'd understood why it would never happen from an early age. It had even brought him to tears occasionally.

    However, Rossiter had long since acknowledged that although he would never be able to be the coach of his beloved team, he would remain a loyal, passionate and fervent supporter until he drew his last breath. Whenever the full-time whistle were to be blown on the professor's life, he would forever bleed black and white.

    With the time now approaching three, Mr. Rossiter grabbed another

beer from the fridge and settled down in front of the screen – as was his long standing Saturday ritual – in anticipation of the game starting. Whenever the team played at home, with the stadium a mere twelve miles from Congletown, Rossiter attended, as he had done for over thirty years. But as today was an away game, he chose to stay at home to watch.
As Clarke felt that all too familiar nervous energy, tension and excitement, he prepared for his team to arrive.

Rossiter was snapped out of his daydreaming by the roar of the crowd on the screen as the players took to the field, led out as always by the captain and talisman, Dom Tope. A local lad and lifelong Fort Dale supporter like Clarke, Topey was an absolute hero to the supporters in these parts. Heroes, however, can only do so much when endeavouring to save the proverbial sinking ship. The team were in poor form on the field and also struggling financially – a predicament that befell the majority of teams playing at Dale's level. Money was often both scarce and unwisely spent, and as such, every team needed someone to save the day. But even Tope wasn't a world – beater, and despite yet another goal and his usual unrivalled work ethic, never say die attitude and love for the shirt, Rossiter's black and white warriors were to lose that afternoon. Again.

With the game over and Clarke disappointed, as he was on a dispiritingly high number of Saturday afternoons, he went to the fridge and got another beer. Win, lose or draw, there was always the consolation of a Playhouse visit, with Carla and Hannah behind the bar.
Happy days.

23.

It was just after eleven when Clarke pushed open the door and duly strode into the bar, acknowledging the staff as he took his usual place at the fabled mahogany. Looking around the room as he sipped on a beer, half price, as all his drinks here were - mates rates and all that - Rossiter realised that he´d yet to say hi to Carla. He would go and see her later. She was always the star attraction, and the main reason for his perhaps too frequent visits to that particular venue. There were quite a few girls about, but the vast majority seemed to already be with guys. After careful deliberation, the professor decided to have another beer before going to the second bar behind the red curtain to talk to Carla. As he swigged on said beverage, he noticed a couple of cute girls glance in his direction with a smile as they effortlessly glided past, presumably in search of their own liquid refreshment. Rossiter generally favoured an attire that was smart casual in nature; tonight he´d opted for jeans, pristine white button down shirt, and a grey blazer to go with a new pair of boots that he´d recently purchased. Clarke didn´t spend a vast amount of money on clothes, yet somehow always managed to look good. He wasn´t a trend setter by any means – revelling more in the pursuit of passion than a slave to fashion – but he always at least made an effort to look the part. A detail that apparently hadn´t gone unnoticed by the beautiful brunette who had sidled past him moments earlier. As she flashed a beaming smile in his direction, Clarke raised his glass to her from across the room in acknowledgement. She was hot, he'd probably introduce himself later. It'd be rude not to...

As he mused, Rossiter was startled out of his distraction by an unexpected beep emanating from his pocket. It was now reasonably late, so he was surprised that anyone should be messaging him at this time. Taking another sip, Congletown's most eligible bachelor withdrew the phone from his pocket to investigate. The message on the screen wasn't what he'd been expecting:

Hi Clarke. I know things between us have been somewhat difficult over the last few months. I probably overreacted to certain things, so I'd like us to clear the air...
Let me know if / when we can talk. It's important to me.
Ana

Clarke could scarcely believe what he was reading. Just as he was finally starting to accept that they had no future together and moving on, with classes now over and her no longer being his student, she'd decided to contact him out of the blue, seemingly with a view to reconciling their differences. It was typical Ana, being moody and dramatic and falling off the radar when things didn't go her way, but then re-initiating contact whenever she felt either lonely, insecure, or needed a favour. Rossiter was pissed off, barely able to disguise his disgust as he sat down at the other bar to talk to Carla. He felt himself almost glaring in spite of himself as he saluted his favourite barmaid, explaining to her surprised face that he was in a bad mood, but that it was through no fault of her own.

"What´s wrong, Clarke? Maybe I can help..."

"Trust me, you can´t. But thanks anyway. A drink would be more than welcome, though."

Without even needing to ask what his poison was, she smiled at Rossiter almost ruefully, before turning away to mix a strong, Spanish style gin and tonic, her beautiful behind pert and perfect in the flustered philanderer´s eyeline. With drink duly mixed, Carla brought it over to Clarke, placing the much needed beverage carefully down upon the bar and he sipped.

"Are you sure you don´t want to tell me what´s wrong? You´re usually so upbeat, so it makes me sad to see you like this."

The forlorn professor looked up from his glass and debated telling her about the entire Analisse fiasco, before hesitantly responding:

"Let´s just call it *girl trouble*..."

The look on Carla´s face was now one of surprise.

"Are you kidding me? I can´t imagine you *ever* having any trouble with the ladies", a smirk and a highly suggestive wink followed.

"You´d better believe it! I really appear to have my work cut out with this one."

Carla smiled again as she turned away to serve a new customer. She had a boyfriend, but Clarke sensed that there could be something between them if he ever decided to make a more concerted effort to take things further. She was staggeringly beautiful, and a really nice girl too. She was good fun, and she made an exemplary g and t. What more could a guy possibly want? When he finally managed to get over Ana, and got tired of fucking the scores of hot but somehow unfulfilling females he continued to attract, he would go all out to try and snare Carla. He owed it to himself.

Having finished his gin and promptly ordering a second, Clarke took his phone from his pocket, stared almost blankly at the screen, and mused over whether or not to reply to Analisse's message. Deciding that it didn't deserve a response – not for the moment at least – Clarke returned the phone and continued to sip. As he turned, he was surprised to see the cute brown haired girl who had smiled at him earlier that night now sitting on the barstool immediately to his right. She turned to face him:

"A man wearing a frown like that *and* drinking gin alone before midnight would raise a red flag to the majority of women. But you look frustrated, sad and in need of company, so I'll take my chances."

Despite feeling both fatigued and pissed off, Rossiter couldn't help a smile from allowing itself to spread across his beleaguered lips.

"Ok, ma lady. Points for the creative and mildly amusing intro. I'll play along. Who might you be?"

"I'm Cristi. Nice to meet you. And you are?"

"I'm Clarke."

"You're also not very talkative. Too much gin will do that to a man. Even one as handsome as you."

Unable to refrain from smiling once more, Clarke put his drink down, turning slightly and offering his hand, which the newcomer seductively shook. As they continued to acquaint themselves with one another and the professor's mood subsequently lightened, she began to intrigue him – not least by virtue of the marked and not unpleasant accent he took heed of as they conversed.

"So, who exactly *are* you, little miss Cristi? From whence might you and your tantalising tongue hail?"

"I´m from Sicily, Italia", she replied, smiling and handing him a free tequila shot that she´d managed to procure from one of the bartenders who was apparently one of her friends. They clinked glasses together, with the sexy Sicilian enthusiastically announcing:

> "Salt, tequila and a slice of lemon.
> Cristi and Clarkey, a match made in heaven!"

More shots followed and they exchanged numbers, with Rossiter´s mood now having changed from one of annoyance in the immediate aftermath of Ana´s unwelcome text message, to enthusiasm and exuberance at having been acquainted with Cristi the intoxicating Italian. She was great fun, a provider of free tequila, and seemed to be an extremely interesting and friendly girl, too. As the conversation progressed, Clarke learned that his new friend was a freelance photographer and artist, and also a part-time barmaid at another venue across town – one that the professor also knew well by virtue of occasional visits there with a former student of his who had since become a dear friend, going by the name of Emiliano Zappa.

With time having flown by and now approaching 3 am, Clarke and Cristi drank one last shot and bade each other goodnight, promising to meet soon for more drinks. She´d told Rossiter during the course of the evening that she was a dab hand with a cocktail shaker, and that her Moscow Mule was the best he´d ever try. So they´d arranged to hang out again – probably the following weekend – as the professor was himself partial to a cocktail and could never turn down an offer like that. He wanted to get to know the caring, smiling Sicilian better, so what better way to start with hard liquor, ice and a slice?

Clarke picked up his coat, smiled at Cristi and – somewhat surprisingly – gave her a hug. This wasn´t usually his modus operandi; he normally attempted at least a kiss when meeting any new girl. But tonight seemed different somehow, *she* seemed different. Caring, warm hearted and loyal, not like many of the girls this young man usually went for. Add in the fact that she appeared to be articulate, intelligent, creative and also pure good fun, and Rossiter was sure that Cristi was a girl worth taking time to get to know properly. Having decided that he needed more fulfilling friendships and relationships with people of integrity in his advancing years, rather than pointless flings with girls in bars, Clarke decided that he would take his time in finding out more about her, in the hope of building a lasting connection. Smiling together as they left the bar, Rossiter hailed a cab and held the door open for her to climb in.

"It was a pleasure meeting you Cristi. I´ll call you next week for drinks. Buonanotte e sogni d´oro!"

"Haha! Ciao Clarke. It was great to meet you, too!"

24.

Clarke stirred sleepily and roused himself from his slumber. The clock on the screen of his phone read 11:00. Long lie-ins the morning after nights of heavy drinking and partying were something of a weekend pattern. Although it were true that his tendency to spend more time than he ought to in bed wasn't always due to fatigue or mere laziness – Rossiter had been an insulin dependent diabetic since the age of six - meaning that his tardiness in waking was occasionally due to his blood sugar levels being lower than usual of a morning, especially if the previous night had been a heavy one, which was the case today. Although sluggish, Clarke could also tell that his sugar was low. Resisting the urge to turn over and continue sleeping, the professor summoned all of his strength to throw back the sheets and get out of bed, heading to the kitchen to get a sugar fix by virtue of a refreshing glass of orange juice. Coffee could wait a while.

The juice was good, both as a means of bolstering sugar levels and rehydration in the face of yet another unwelcome weekend hangover. Rossiter set the glass aside, and looked again at Analisse's message from the previous evening. Puffing out his cheeks as he deliberated over the best course of action to take, Clarke decided that any decision would have to wait until after brunch. He wrestled a frying pan from the cupboard in which to make some scrambled eggs, which was also Ana's brunch of choice, and one that Rossiter had made for her on more than one occasion, and set about the task. Last night's message had irked him, probably more than he'd expected it to. Now he couldn't even make breakfast without her edging her way into his head. She had a way of doing that; of being present at the most inopportune times, and often when Clarke didn't want her there. He decided that the situation needed to be dealt with once and for all, but that a brief text message wouldn't cut it as a means of response. There was still so much that Rossiter wanted and needed to get off his chest in order to get what women – often feminists – irritatingly referred to as *closure*. That afternoon, he sat down with a beer after brunch and wrote Ana an email:

Ana,

Hard to believe that it's been only a few short months since we met. Meeting at the Playhouse, and oh my, that red dress! Enough to drive a man crazy.

Then, as though our fleeting inebriated meetings weren't enough, we unknowingly became teacher and student. Almost as though the world was conspiring against us, in some way. I know it may sound silly, but from the moment during our very first class together when you got up and closed the door, shuffling back to your seat and offering that most sheepish of smiles, I knew that there was something different about you. Something unusual. I don't really know why, but I simply knew that I had to find out more...

Yes, you were a gifted student, and I sincerely hope that you will continue to progress and have the success that you undoubtedly deserve, regardless of whatever the future may hold for you. But whatever may come to pass, I want and need you to know that I am grateful for every single moment that we have spent together; from that closing of classroom doors that signalled a venture into the unknown, then that first real conversation that we had after class, as teacher and student, and as 'friends`. Talking on that afternoon – for the first time in real depth – will be a moment that I will never forget. I mean that sincerely.

And then we come to everything that's happened since. At this point I really need to make it clear that in all the different situations that we've been involved in together: drinker and drinkee, teacher and student, or two forsaken lovers, I have always seen you as a truly remarkable human being. A flawed and vulnerable one at times – as am I – but no matter. I suppose what I'm trying to say is that I have always respected you – and always will – be that as a bar-goer, student, or just as the intelligent, quirky, intriguing and breathtakingly beautiful woman that you are. I've never been one for being shallow and / or sycophantic; but there should be a statue of you in that red dress!

Anyway, that's enough verbatim. For a man supposedly at ease with the written word, I seem to use a lot of them – and not always wisely!

So I will cut to the chase; the main purpose of this email is to tell you that, for as much as I would love for things to be different, whatever we have or indeed have had, ends here. Now.

You told me that we cannot be together, because we are both disabled.

Whether that be the only reason for reluctance on your part to engage in further 'beasting of the two backs' following our initial encounters, I know not. But whether or not other reasons exist for your inability or unwillingness to take things further with me, this situation cannot continue as it is.

I love you, Ana. I loved you from the very first moment I ever set eyes on you and as a consequence, I simply cannot only be 'friends' with you. To accept such a fate would be like agreeing to some sort of consolation prize.
So here endeth the story of you and I, Analisse. I am absolutely heartbroken writing these words to you. Saying goodbye to you – and it truly has to be goodbye – will be the most difficult thing I have ever had to do. But in protecting both myself, and more importantly, you, so it must be. It is with a heavy heart, that I bid you farewell.

I love you, Ana. More than you will ever know.

Clarke

25.

Upon finishing the final sentence and reluctantly hitting send, a single, solemn tear escaped from each of Rossiter's eyes and meandered morosely down his pallid cheeks. Despite feeling a sadness akin to sheer devastation, the professor knew that he had done the right thing in sending that most emotional of messages. He'd been disappointed by his failures with the so-called 'fairer' sex on more occasions than he cared to remember, but this felt entirely different. As Clarke had gradually become better with women following the female fuelled frustrations of his teenage years and subsequently as a young adult, eventually having decided that enough was enough and making the conscious decision to improve that area of his life, he made such huge progress that although he still experienced occasional knock-backs from women, they were few and far between. Now in his thirties, Rossiter found it much easier to rationalise these rejections. And even though he still got mildly frustrated on the rare occasions that an especially hot woman rebuffed his advances, he merely put it down to one missed opportunity among many that always came his way. Picking up women was a numbers game, and Clarke had gone to painstaking lengths to succeed in that part of his life that had been a source of such chagrin as he'd been growing up. It had been an arduous journey, one during which he'd had to do much soul searching. But thanks to his gargantuan efforts, he finally succeeded in becoming the charismatic, respectable ladies' man that he'd wanted to be for as long as he could remember. It wasn't a fight that the majority of men ever chose to take on. Things with women were now so *easy* for him – that wasn't arrogance, merely a fact – that the challenge had been worth it.

Forcing himself to bid farewell to Analisse Lejeune, however, would doubtless prove more difficult than any of the professor's previous failed amorous adventures. He had never known *anyone* like her, but he knew it couldn't continue. Getting over her would be painful, but at least he could stop torturing himself and get a clean break. Writing the final email had proved somewhat cathartic, even though Clarke was almost certain that Ana wouldn't even dignify it with a response. Temperamental and volatile as she so often was, mademoiselle would doubtless see it as Clarke being selfish, immature even. When they had been *just good friends*, Ana had had everything she'd wanted and needed from him; friendship, help, emotional support and a shoulder to cry on whenever she required it. She got everything out of their 'arrangement`, but what about what Clarke wanted? Ana had been having her cake and eating it for far too long. She wasn't a bad person – Clarke wouldn't have fallen for her so hard otherwise – but she took him for granted. The worst thing was that Rossiter wasn't sure that Ana even *realised* it. The email was the most suitable way to bring their story to a sad but necessary end.

Clarke went to sit outside in the afternoon sunshine. As he sat on the bandstand, he looked to his left and saw Peruvian neighbour sexy Lexi outside on her terrace. God, those shorts were tight. But he didn't really acknowledge her, he had more important things on his mind, like where the next much needed beer was coming from. He ambled to the fridge to find one.

Making his way back to the terrace, Clarke heard a distant buzz emanate from his laptop in the living room. It sounded like the video messaging service, probably his mum trying to call him for one of their frequent catch-ups. Rossiter loved, admired and respected his mother more than anybody else in the entire world; but the beer tasted so good, and the lovely Linda wouldn't stress if he tarded slightly in calling her back. The living room seemed incredibly far away at this moment in time, so he would enjoy the beer and sunshine, and be sure to contact her later.

When he eventually made his way indoors, however, Clarke realised that it hadn't been his mother attempting to make a call. It had been none other than Ana. He sat down just in time for the online messenger to start ringing again. Feeling surprised more than anything else, the professor clicked answer. The sight that greeted him wasn't what he'd been expecting. Analisse was red faced, incandescent, and sobbing into her webcam like a sullen child:

"What the *hell* was that email, Clarke?!" she screamed, her teary eyes staring straight ahead, almost as though she were looking *through* the screen, imploring him to answer. When he hesitated briefly in order to compose his thoughts before answering – a delay that couldn't have been more than two seconds at most – the furious Frenchy slammed an impatient fist upon the table in front of her in anticipation of his response.

"Listen, Ana, I thought the email was the best way – perhaps the *only* way – to articulate my feelings clearly with minimal drama for both of us."

"So you thought you could just walk out of my life, and not even do it in person?! A fucking email? Is that all you think I'm worth, Clarke?! All I deserve?!"

Now it was Rossiter's turn to get irate:

"Now hold it right there! My decision to do this by email has absolutely nothing to do with what I think you're *worth*! You know exactly what I feel for you, and I'm insulted that you would think otherwise. This is precisely the kind of reaction I'd been hoping to avoid! Every time I've tried to talk to you about my feelings face to face, it's culminated in tension, shouting, arguments. So in choosing to send an email, I was – hard though it may be for you to comprehend – endeavouring to protect us both. But it appears that all it's done is provoke yet another childish tantrum on your behalf! I've already told you that things can't continue as they are. I'm simply looking for a clean break. That's just the way it has to be, Ana."

She looked back at him, mouth now open, incredulous:

"But you can't just walk out of my life, Clarke! I *need* you!"

"That's the problem though, Analisse! It's always what *you* want, what *you* need! I'm sorry, but enough is enough. I need to start thinking about myself. I'm sorry that it's come to this... devastated in fact. But that's the way it has to be. I wish you all the very best for the future, and I will never forget you. But now it's time to go our separate ways..."

As Ana looked back at the screen, she covered her face with both hands and began sobbing uncontrollably once more. Although Clarke had tried to remain composed for the duration of what had predictably been an incredibly difficult situation, the fact that he and this amazing young woman had now come to the end of what had been both an enlightening and immensely tricky road to navigate, caused a solitary tear to escape from each eye and roll down his cheeks in a desolate descent. He wearily dragged the mouse and clicked to end the call.

It was over.

26.

The most difficult part was done. Heartbreaking though losing Analisse was – he probably wouldn´t feel the full ramifications of his actions until a few days or weeks hence – Clarke knew that he had taken the necessary steps to be able to close that chapter of his life, turn the page, and begin penning new ones, both figuratively and literally. His part – time writing projects had been somewhat neglected of late, not least as a consequence of all the drama with Ana. Now Rossiter could use his scribblings as a means of distraction, something to take his mind off all the unwanted upheaval.

His latest beer was getting unsurprisingly tepid, having been left in the sun while he´d been bearing his soul to miss Lejeune. He slurped it down, almost grimacing as he did so, wiping his mouth with the back of his hand and going to get another one. As it was Saturday afternoon, his beloved Fort Dale were in action again, and kick-off time was fast approaching, which meant more beers. He would settle down in front of his computer and watch live, the same as he did every Saturday. His stepfather, Tray Williams, was one of the summarisers for the local radio station, so not only was Clarke able to watch his beloved team from afar, but there was also the added bonus of in-depth analysis and the occasional joke between Tray and his radio colleagues. After the usual ninety minutes of nervous nail biting, Dale triumphed 0-1 away from home, courtesy yet again of star player Tope heading home a late winner. Tonight was going to be fun, a celebration of a much - needed three points.

    Clarke would almost certainly go to the Playhouse later. But first, he headed downstairs and across the road to the One Euro Bar, a mere fifteen yards from his front door. The bar owed its name to the fact that a beer cost only one pound or euro - both currencies were accepted - and there were many of its type in the neighbourhood.

The One Euro Bar was unlike any other that Rossiter had ever frequented. Upon arrival in the district a few years earlier, he´d noticed the small, unremarkable looking bar across the street, and had gone over for a beer and to introduce himself to the locals. Being new to the area, he felt as though he needed to acquaint himself with them as quickly as possible, and with beer being so ridiculously cheap, it was the perfect fuel to get chatting with people in his new surroundings.

    They were certainly an eccentric bunch. First there was Minguet, a raging alcoholic in his early sixties who was at the bar – and in the same chair – every single day, from soon after the doors opened at 7 am, until he staggered home wearily content at around 9 pm. Since Rossiter had moved to the area, he´d always been amazed how Minguet – and a handful of the One Euro Bar´s other patrons – managed to drink such vast quantities of alcohol on a daily basis. Yes, Clarke enjoyed a drink – perhaps too much so at times – but compared to the amount that these guys put away, he could be deemed little more than a social drinker. Their consumption was truly incredible.

Then there was Pep, a corpulent, jovial fellow who drank considerably less than many of the other customers, but still chose to hang around the bar for much of the day. Living just across the street, he could be seen there at regular intervals, wandering from table to table and talking to the regulars as they sipped on their cheap beer. Pep, like many of One Euro's customers, was retired. He'd lived in the neighbourhood his whole life, as was the case for the majority. It was a working class part of town, and for most of these loyal patrons, it was all they'd ever known. It wasn't an exciting bar, and Rossiter only rarely set foot in there, mainly due to the fact that there was a dearth of hot women. The One Euro Bar was very much a place for local people, most of whom were either retired or unemployed, and weren't interested in venturing outside of their comfort zone, preferring to stick to the status quo and drink in the welcoming but decidedly dull bubble that they'd been frequenting and socialising in their entire lives. It amazed Rossiter that they never seemed to get bored, heading over the road on a daily basis for beers and chit chat, the very essence of familiarity and routine. It was all they knew.

There were other drinkers there who Clarke now considered good friends. There was Johann – or Saint Michael, as he was later nicknamed – by virtue of his fondness for famous Spanish beers. And the wonderfully named 'More the Face', a retired plumber and seasoned traveller in his mid sixties who jetted off around the world on regular holidays, paid for by his generous pension and various property sales. Despite his comfortable financial situation, however, More the Face almost never bought anybody a drink. He was jovial and a good man, yet decidedly stingy, and would often make politically incorrect comments about the other patrons after a couple of glasses of red. It went without saying that he always ordered the cheapest wine available, never failing to quibble over a few measly pennies when the time came to settle his tab.

Hence, the One Euro Bar was certainly a place unlike any other, but it was now very familiar to Rossiter despite his visits there having become much less frequent of late. The customers were humble, hard working people for the most part. The fact that Clarke was a professor meant that he was a source of intrigue for them. Although there were a few shady characters, Clarke admired their friendliness and work ethic, and he could relate to them, even if they had little in common apart from their love of drink.

Clarke limited himself to two beers, and having indulged in the usual pleasantries with a handful of the bar's regulars, duly said his goodbyes and returned home in preparation for yet another Playhouse visit. It turned out to be fairly uneventful, and he prepared to leave after a brief chat with a cute new barmaid and the customary two gin and tonics. Rossiter always marvelled at how drinks were served in this particular bar; there was at least twice as much alcohol in any long drink than elsewhere, whether it be whiskey, gin, or another spirit. Drinks here were rocket fuel, and had to be sipped at a leisurely pace, especially given the fact that the professor's drinks were even stronger, by virtue of his being acquainted with the Playhouse staff.

Finishing his final drink and bidding farewell to the array of beautiful barmaids, Rossiter took his cane and jacket from behind the bar and made for the door to hail a cab from the usual place at the end of the street. Despite not having drunk that much, Clarke felt surprisingly tired, without being entirely sure why. He supposed that it was a culmination of that afternoon's Analisse drama, followed by yet another nerve – wracking Dale game, topped off with a quantity of booze which, although not excessive, had become the norm for a Saturday. Being uncharacteristically fatigued, he hadn't even attempted to talk to any women or get any phone numbers, and as the taxi dropped him off outside, he trooped wearily to the front door and collapsed into the nearest available chair, letting out a long, almost beleaguered sigh as he did so.

Clarke poured himself a glass of red and mused over the events of the last few days. The Analisse saga was now over, but Rossiter was still physically and mentally exhausted, which was undoubtedly why he hadn´t even attempted to pull any new girls that night. Women were truly wonderful creatures, but for the time being, he would focus on taking care of himself and putting his own interests above all else. His writing had certainly taken a back seat of late, and he needed to remedy that. For all that Rossiter lived as carefree and relaxed a life as possible, he still needed something to focus on. Writing was his best way of staying grounded, lucid. The power of the pen was a welcome distraction when other areas of his life went off the rails – which they occasionally did – and he still found a certain reassurance in getting the creative juices flowing.

Writing had always played a role in Rossiter's life that could be deemed somewhat unusual, contradictory even. The term *career* was one that Clarke had always employed loosely, especially with regard to writing, which was always something he'd seen more as a hobby than a means of paying the bills. His family weren't particularly big readers, save for his mother indulging in the odd paperback to pass the time on any given sun - drenched beach holiday. Rossiter's family had never discouraged his writing, but they'd always seen it merely as one of his hobbies. They'd been somewhat surprised when, after many years of toying with the idea, Clarke had announced that he had recently begun writing his first serious novel. Their attitude seemed to be to let him get on with it, if it was something he enjoyed, but none of his immediate family had seemed to set much store in writing as a viable career path. So, whilst his wish to pen something meaningful was never sneered at or discouraged, they just didn't seem to think it would go anywhere.

The professor had never seen teaching as his future career, either. Educating other people was something he'd just kind of stumbled into, rather than actively sought. During his year abroad, that fabulous first year living in France during his university days, he had chosen to be a Language Assistant, teaching English to French teenagers in one of the secondary schools in the beautiful city which was to become his new home. The French adventure was one that had almost never happened at all, however. The university staff had warned Clarke that although a year abroad was mandatory for all students of foreign languages, he may not be able to go, as they were struggling to find a school that would agree to having an assistant with a physical disability. The young Rossiter had been perturbed by this revelation, not least because the chance to do paid work abroad had been one of the main reasons for his having chosen that particular course of study. Not being able to test himself both personally and professionally on foreign shores would have been a real slap in the face. But the university staff pulled out all the stops in managing to find a school willing to allow Clarke to work with them, and so his first steps on the career path were taken. Even now, however, with many years´ teaching experience under his belt, Rossiter still saw it as something that he had *ended up* doing, rather than actively chosen. He had a good rapport with the vast majority of his students, but he didn´t see himself as a pedagogue. He enjoyed teaching – most of the time – but it wasn´t his true passion. That dubious honour fell to football, and more specifically his beloved Fort Dale. There had only ever been one job that Clarke truly longed to do, and that was to be Fort Dale manager. He felt that it was his true calling, but alas, it could never be so. He´d had to be incredibly strong to get over that disappointment. It had taken him years to accept the fact that he would never be able to do the only job that really, *truly* mattered to him. But as time passed, he acknowledged the fact that rather than being beaten by heartbreak not of his own making, he had to go in search of other opportunities. Languages and teaching had opened different doors, and the professor was grateful for the life that they had helped him to forge for himself. Rossiter had always had to struggle and fight for everything that he had achieved, and with the help of his friends and family, especially his mother, he had overcome the odds yet again. So, yes he enjoyed teaching, but he also needed to get back to writing. As he finished his glass of wine, he yawned and headed to bed. Write he would, but not tonight.

27.

A few weeks had passed since the last goodbye with Analisse. It was Sunday, and Clarke rose at a surprisingly respectable hour, had a leisurely breakfast and sat down to put pen to paper. He was at a loss as to what to write, or at least he *had* been. This particular weekend had been a strange one, however. One of the strangest of his – and indeed most people 's entire life.

Congletown, the whole country – and indeed most of the world – had been placed on lockdown by its respective governments, in a bid to combat a new virus that had allegedly originated on the other side of the world, and had now spread and become highly contagious across the globe. The Colonavirus was at large and rampant. Supermarket shelves were bare, and the planet's irrational panic was spreading as rapidly as the virus itself.

Despite repeated pleas by the authorities for citizens not to indulge in panic buying, the procurement of so-called *essential* items was easier said than done. Government legislation had ordained that citizens across the globe only be permitted to leave their homes to go to supermarkets, to obtain vital medication on prescription, or to walk their dogs. In the majority of countries, even daily perambulations or other forms of exercise had been temporarily outlawed, owing to the increasing velocity with which the voracious, seemingly insatiable Novid-19 virus was spreading. Numbers of cases and fatalities were increasing at an alarming rate, on a daily basis, and even paying a visit to one's family and friends was now strictly forbidden. The situation was becoming increasingly grave, with people rushing to supermarkets and stockpiling products which were often far from essential. In the early days of this wholly unanticipated pandemic, even the most basic provisions were becoming worryingly rare commodities, with paranoid shoppers piling their trolleys high with excessive amounts of toilet paper and other everyday items. Alcohol sales were rocketing, however. So, while everyone was able to get drunk if they so desired, a selfish and moronic minority were making the wiping of one's backside an increasingly fanciful longing for the majority of a now panic – stricken, increasingly impoverished population.

There were, however, positives to come out of the pandemic. Amidst all the panic, worry and stress, people were united in attempting to overcome the crisis. Healthcare professionals were risking their lives to help the afflicted and were duly applauded for their heroics all around the world. In Rossiter's neighbourhood, 8 pm was when all the neighbours came out onto balconies and doorsteps, cheering, clapping and saluting the efforts of those who were risking everything to help others. The sense of unity and bonding was discernible not only in Congletown, but all around the world. Indeed, Rossiter's mother had baked a cake for all of the neighbours to have a piece of on one particular clapathon. As a radiographer herself, she was currently unable to work due to injury. But she understood all too well the risks being taken by medical workers in fighting the battle on the front line. Needless to say that Linda's cake was baked with a smile and devoured by her grateful neighbours with gusto. She always had a knack of doing something kind in a bid to bring people together and boost the community's morale.

Being on lockdown wasn't particularly a hardship for Rossiter. All classes for himself and his Congletown University colleagues were now being taught online as the pandemic took hold. He didn't mind this, however. It was exactly the same work, but now he could do it from the comfort of his own home. The dynamics of on-site and online classes were different. It went without saying that Clarke enjoyed being in a classroom, as it allowed him to interact with the students in an ambience that was more personal, and therefore enjoyable. But in spite of that, on balance, he still preferred working from home. Okay, he didn't live particularly far from his place of work. But the daily walk was often sapping, especially given that he didn't finish teaching until late most evenings, which meant that by the time he got home, all he had time for was a quick bite to eat and a couple of drinks to unwind before bed.

Hence, the new system of working from home that companies, schools and universities had been forced to adopt, during this period where the entire planet was on edge, suited Rossiter. He often felt somewhat bemused when reading online comments from people who were 'going out of their mind' with being forced to stay at home. People frequently complained of having too much work, or being stressed out during confinement with children and spouses. Depending on which reports one decided to read, domestic violence levels were on the up. Rossiter had initially found such statistics strange; upon reflection, however, when he imagined what it would be like for him to be on lockdown with some of the nutcase women he'd dated at certain times of his life, he began to take a more tolerant, considered view of the strains that people, families and couples may be under, and thanked his lucky stars that he was living alone during this period of confinement. The last thing he would've wanted would be to have some crazy chick – however gifted she may be between the sheets – driving him insane.

As far as work was concerned, the professor was adapting to the new online regime, and even rather enjoying it. Some people talked of missing regular human contact, craving interaction with others on a daily basis, something which had now abruptly been taken away. This wasn't the case for Clarke, however. The majority of his colleagues at Congletown were very pleasant and personable, but he couldn't really say that he *missed* them. There were a few cute female teachers, but nobody that tickled his fancy more than usual.

As entertaining as the occasional sending of messages could be, it wasn't the same as actually being with people in what might be deemed a normal, everyday environment. In much the same way as Clarke had initially found it strange teaching online, the virus was having a similar effect upon inter – personal relationships, and consequently, interactions between men and women. In a modern world where social media and dating apps were increasingly beginning to dick – tate the ways in which members of both sexes were meeting and choosing whether or not to embark upon potential relationships, the pandemic appeared to be a cause of increased loneliness and even anxiety, brought about by an imposed need to isolate. Being forced to distance oneself from friends, family and any other individuals for the foreseeable future had perhaps unsurprisingly led to increased use of social media, applications and the like, as people attempted to reconnect in whatever way possible. Ever the cynic, it struck Rossiter as somewhat ironic that in a modern world which, particularly for teenagers and twenty somethings, revolved almost exclusively around mobile phones and online activity, people were complaining or sometimes even panicking about having to interact through social media, in the midst of an imposed lack of face – to – face communication. For today´s youngsters, whose entire world seemed to hinge upon a swipe here, a like or a click there, the fact that so many of them appeared resigned to solitude and depressed by at not being able to see loved ones, spoke volumes. Teenagers and young adults frequently alluded to boredom and even stress as a consequence of their unexpected isolation. While the professor acknowledged that anybody could potentially get bored, and that stress and other mental health issues of course had to be taken seriously, as the pandemic´s stranglehold tightened and showed no sign of abating, he was saddened – even astounded – that in a world where there was an abundance of technology and entertainment, young people were finding it so difficult to occupy themselves.

    Dating had been made more difficult too, of course. Since

lockdown had begun, Clarke had only been able to go out to the supermarket or pharmacy. So by default, as much as he preferred to meet women in person, with that option now off the table for the foreseeable future, he had been forced to content himself with swipes and likes as a means of coming into contact with new women. Indeed, he had made contact with a couple of new girls and exchanged a few messages, but it wasn´t the same as real dating. Rossiter was happy enough working from home, but he was starting to miss ass more than class. Post pandemic, the professor´s pursuit of new pussy would be relentless.

He had just finished the latest batch of online lessons and was relaxing on the sofa with a hard-earned evening beer, when his phone beeped. He was surprised, as he wasn´t expecting any textual correspondence, especially at this tardy hour. Surprise became disbelief when he saw that the name on the screen was none other than Analisse Lejeune. They hadn´t communicated for a number of weeks since their emails, video call and subsequent parting of ways, so Clarke was somewhat bemused as to why she may be contacting him now. Rossiter´s younger brother was getting married in Italy just a few weeks hence, and the professor had that on his mind, rather than another dispute with the Frenchy. Maybe in these strange, virus – ridden times, she was reconnecting with him with a view to acquiring a seat on the plane to sunnier climes. Clarke had mentioned the wedding to Ana in a previous conversation, so she knew it was happening.

Rossiter sipped his beer and contemplated how to handle the fanciable Frenchy´s unexpected return. After careful deliberation – and three more beers – Clarke decided that he had to take action. In much the same way as Congletown and the entire world was embroiled in a battle with Novid – 19, the professor needed to make sure that any potential reconnection with Analisse Lejeune didn't turn into a virus of a different kind that might endeavour to suck the life out of the faculty's favourite fellow. He clicked to read her message:

Hi Clarke,
I know we parted ways a while ago now, but I hate it.
I hate the way things ended, and that we don't talk anymore.
The world is fucking crazy! Especially now that this shitty virus has taken hold!
I was supposed to meet with a friend tonight, but she didn't want to flout lockdown rules. But I don't care! I'm at the end of your street, and I want to see you! I need to!

Rossiter could hardly believe what he was reading. Here she was, resurfacing after having practically forced the professor to cut her adrift in a bid to save his own sanity and emotional well – being, and she was apparently in the neighbourhood! It was so typical of Ana, that he didn't know whether to laugh, applaud or scream. It was almost as though she had some kind of radar; a device capable of seeking him out, pushing his buttons and preying upon his weaknesses with a view to entrapping him whenever she saw fit.

He glanced at his phone screen again, disgusted with himself as much as with her as he walked slowly to the door to let her in.

Analisse was standing two metres away from the professor´s front door, in keeping with social distancing rules, waiting impatiently with hands on hips as Clarke opened and invited her in with a sweeping hand gesture. She glided past him with an irritated expression on her face, looking him up and down with a scowl before sitting down in the living room, tutting in disapproval at the beer cans strewn across the table.

"Some things never change. Jesus, Clarke! When are you going to sort your life out?"

"You can stop that right now! I mean it, Ana! You´ve only been in my house for a matter of seconds, and you´re already looking down your nose at me, being all holier than thou! What business is it of yours if I choose to have a few beers after a hard day´s graft?"

Analisse chuckled under her breath, almost seeming to sneer at Rossiter´s pitifully weak attempt to justify and rationalise what she deemed to be an existence which was apparently becoming increasingly devoid of any true purpose or meaning. Clarke had always struck Ana as the type of guy who did exactly what he wanted, and lived life on his own terms. It was precisely that – seductive smile notwithstanding – that had attracted her to him. But this was different. They hadn´t seen one another for a considerable time now, but the more weeks and months passed, the more it seemed to Analisse that the professor was living his life with almost reckless abandon. He was on the brink, it seemed to her, and it made her sad. She had been absolutely devastated when Clarke had decided that they should no longer stay in contact, the emotional video call a few months previously had been testament to that.

But she had decided that although they couldn't be together, she didn't want to let him walk out of her life completely. Yes, his attitude to life sometimes annoyed and frustrated her, but she nevertheless found it – and him – attractive in the extreme. It was for that very reason that she had decided that she would attempt to reconnect with him and build bridges. At the risk of opening old wounds, she felt it had to be done. Even though they had already slept together, Analisse wanted to try and be friends with him. She sat down on the sofa and turned to face Clarke:

"I know we agreed that we should part ways a few months ago, but I don't want to. I thought I would be able to get used to the idea, but I can't."

"Ok, but what exactly is it that you're looking for? I thought that by cutting ties, we could both move on. I was starting to do just that. Evidently, that's not the case for you..."

"Listen, Clarke, I don't want to keep going over old ground every time we have a disagreement. I was really upset when you decided that we should go our separate ways, but you gave me no choice. You did what you thought was best, and I tried to respect your wishes and deal with the situation. But having been through everything we've been through, and all the intensity, pressure and stress that went with it... it was just too much, too intense. But from that, to not having you in my life at all... well... I can't deal with that. I thought I would get used to not having you around, but I can't. I want you in my life, but only as a friend, nothing more."

Clarke looked directly at Ana, bemused. It seemed as though she wanted to have her cake and eat it, but Rossiter still wasn't sure he could accept only being friends with her. Too much had already happened; there was too much baggage, too much history. The professor's logical brain was telling him that mere friendship was no longer an option. He knew all too well that once the slightest hint of physical attraction or feelings entered the fray, there was no turning back. The fact that Clarke and Analisse had built such a strong emotional and physical connection meant that the idea of them being just friends was almost absurd to him. Logically, he knew that he should reject the notion completely, tell her that just being buddies wasn't enough for him, and that he should show her the door, and never look back. The problem was that logic went out of the window where Clarke and Ana were concerned. He turned to face her again:

"Listen, Ana. I won't lie to you. I never have, and I won't start now. I'm not sure that being just friends is going to be possible for me. But if it's what you want, we can give it a go..."

Rossiter was almost kicking himself even as he was saying it. He had always been so sure of what he wanted with all the women he allowed into his life. He had a clear idea of boundaries, of what he would and wouldn't accept. But Analisse always seemed to *weaken* him in some way. He always felt so in control in his personal and professional life, and he despised himself for being such a pushover where she was concerned. It always seemed to be about what *she* wanted, what was best for *her*. She was a nice girl, but selfish at times, and Clarke loathed himself for indulging her... again. Analisse looked unsurprisingly satisfied – almost smug – as she replied:

"Great! Let´s just put the past and all the drama behind us, and focus on being friends. It was all too intense before, so I´m glad you´ve decided to change your mind. Haha! It´s almost like I can persuade you to do anything I want..." she said, with a wink and a little giggle as she looked at Clarke, evidently pleased with herself.

Rossiter didn´t quite know what to make of this latest development. He had genuinely believed that they would have been permanently out of one another´s lives by now, so his begrudging U-turn was something of a turn-up for the books. He glanced distractedly around the living room, rubbing his now clammy hands over his face in an attempt to find a way to proceed with the conversation. Putting his hands on the arm of the chair and wearily walking towards the living room door, he turned to Ana.

"Drink? You´re here anyway, and it´s pretty much apéro time already. You may as well stay so we can talk things through. I guess that´s what friends do, right?"

Ana briefly glanced at her phone, "yeah, ok then. I´ve still got a couple of things to do later, but I suppose a quick drink won´t hurt. I´ll have a Mojito, please, when you´re ready!"

That was so typical of her, just assuming that he had all the right ingredients and would make any drink she desired at the drop of a hat. Although this aspect of Ana´s personality still irked Clarke at times, he was becoming so used to the Frenchy´s whims that he was almost immune to that side of her by now. There never seemed to be any middle ground with Analisse Lejeune, she did everything to the extreme; from sweet, naïve and almost childlike at times, sometimes an absolute diva who expected everything to be provided for her with a click of the fingers, and then the other extreme, the tempestuous temptress who could fly off the handle at any given moment, almost wailing like a banshee as she flew into one of her often terrifying tantrums. For now, though, Ana was in diva mode; she knew that Clarke having agreed to their being friends again meant that he had succumbed to her, just as he had done so many times in the past. The professor believed that Ana thought she was better than him, and it riled him sometimes, but he had known for a long time now that she would never change. The fact that even though he knew all of her failings he nevertheless accepted them – and her – was perhaps what annoyed the young man most of all.

  He shuffled into the kitchen and began preparing miss Lejeune's Mojito. As he took the mint, lime, sugar, soda and white rum out of the cupboard – he had all the requisite ingredients, as he regularly made cocktails both for himself and any girls he brought back to his place who had slightly more exotic tastes – he mixed away, preparing the minty refreshment. Making fancy drinks always reminded him of his good friend Stan Pleasures. It had been a while since he´d caught up with Stan. He would call him later, once the latest Analisse tornado had swirled out of town.

  Clarke went back into the living room with Ana´s Mojito and a beer for himself and sat down next to her on the sofa, taking a thirst-quenching sip of cerveza as he gathered his thoughts.

  "So... any plans for the spring and summer months?" was all he could muster.

"Not much, to be honest. Just gonna hang out with family and friends, chill at home, enjoy the holidays. Nothing special. How about you?" Rossiter cleared his throat hesitantly, almost nervously as he appeared flustered in attempting to formulate a response to what seemed a pretty straightforward question:

"Well, my little brother´s getting married in Italy at the end of May. It´s only a couple of weeks away, and there´s still so much that needs to be sorted out."

"I can imagine. You and your older brother are best men, if I remember correctly?"

"Yeah, that´s right. I´m not writing anything too long, though. Contrary to popular belief, speeches aren´t really my forte. I decided to write a poem instead. Finished it last night, actually."

Ana raised her eyebrows at this, though probably more in anticipation than surprise. She knew all too well that Rossiter was quite the master craftsman in both the written and spoken word – some of his musings in the past about literature and a wide range of other subjects had seemed so impassioned and grandiose as to be almost Shakespearian at times – so she looked forward to hearing what he would deliver at the wedding.

The ceremony was to take place in Sorrento at the end of May. Rossiter was in two minds about asking Analisse to join him on his first ever trip to Italy. It was something he was really looking forward to, and having the delectable miss Lejeune on his arm would add a little extra sparkle to what would already be a spectacular event. A whole host of family and friends would be there, including a select bunch of both Dom (the groom) and Pat (Clarke′s older brother′s) friends. It was sure to be quite the party, and everyone was excited about the lead up to the wedding, and the big day itself. But there was still much to be organised. Although the professor was undeniably keen on having Ana as his plus one for a week of Lamborghinis, Martinis and (hopefully) cunniling-uini, it was potentially risky. Beni Rothwell had recently encouraged Clarke to ask Ana to go with him as they′d sipped drinks together after one of her Playhouse shifts, saying that he needed to pull out all the stops to ensure that she got on that plane with him, and that he would regret it if he didn′t have her by his side. Not everybody was of the same opinion, however, with several people sounding a note of caution at the prospect of Analisse – Rossiter′s former student, no less – joining him on the flight to Naples and subsequent week – long sunny sojourn. Her mother had herself told Clarke – Mrs. Lejeune′s face has unexpectedly swooped onto the screen when Rossiter and Ana had been in the middle of a video call – that he would be ill advised to take her darling daughter with him on the trip, such was the ambiguity surrounding their relationship. Ana′s friends also had misgivings about the Italian adventure, suggesting that he merely saw it as an opportunity to *have his way* with her. As such, Ana was starting to have doubts about going with Clarke. The professor, however, was now absolutely clear about wanting her to be there. He looked once again at her, staring expectantly into those beautiful blue eyes, almost imploring her to accept the invitation to go with him on the trip of a lifetime.

"Come on Ana, come with me to the wedding! It′s going to be absolutely fantastic! Neither of us have ever been to Italy, and it′ll be an unforgettable experience, I promise you!"

Analisse looked nervously around the room, before composing herself with a sip of Mojito:

"I´m tempted, Clarke, I really am. But my friends and my mum don´t think it´d be a good idea. I don´t want there to be any confusion or ambiguity about our situation. We can only be friends, nothing more. I´m worried that if I agree to go with you, you might get the wrong idea. Sorrento sounds fantastic, and I´m sure you´ll have a great time, even if I´m not there..."

Clarke really wanted Ana with him on the plane, but he wouldn´t beg. That ´d never been his style. He took another swig of beer, subsequently feeling much calmer, before replying:

"Sure. I understand why you might be having doubts, and I certainly won ´t be putting any pressure on you. I also comprehend your family and friends´ reasons for being unsure about the whole thing. They´re just trying to look after you. The only thing I will say, is that I have to book the tickets in two weeks, maximum. It can´t be any later than that, as time is already of the essence. So, here´s what I suggest: if we talk and hang out a few times over the next two weeks, and everything goes well and you decide you do want to come with me, I will book two tickets faster than you can say no nipples in Naples! No pressure from me. Think about it carefully over the next fortnight, take your time, and I will respect your decision, whatever it may be. Do we have a deal, bella?"

Rossiter flashed a warm, friendly smile towards her, making Ana feel comfortable, safe and secure in an instant, just as he always seemed able to.

    The professor finished a final mouthful of beer and crushed the can in the palm of his hand, lifting himself up off the couch to go in search of another. He gestured to Analisse with another smile and hand gesture, to enquire as to whether she wanted another Mojito.

"Hey, think of all that fantastic wine we´ll be having if you *do* decide to come to Italia! And Limoncello too, lemony liquor of the gods, I tell you! But while your tastebuds are being tantalised with that veritable vision of the vita bella, first to more pressing matters: another Mojito, missy?" Analisse seemed to hesitate slightly, doubtless tempted by more mintiness, before declining. She had things she needed to do this evening and in the coming days, not least weigh up whether or not the offer of a trip to Sorrento had come at the right momento...

28.

    It was now later in May, and already surprisingly warm for the time of year. Analisse was sitting in the mid-morning sunshine by the swimming pool at her parents´ house, sipping thoughtfully on a cup of Springton´s tea. She always drank it *English style* now, with milk, just as Rossiter had encouraged her to. She chuckled as she thought back to the first time they´d indulged in the nation´s most famous hot beverage together, when Ana had looked aghast upon seeing Rossiter pour milk into his brew, swirling the brown-white cloudiness around with a nonchalant flick of the spoon.

"What?! How can you drink tea with milk in?! Ils sont fous ces Anglais!"

"It's the best way to drink tea. You've got to have milk in, no question! Go on, have a taste. I reckon you'll like it!"

So Ana had taken Clarke up on his offer and had a sip. Surprisingly, she *did* in fact like it, and from that point on, never drank it black again. Taking another sip and putting the mug down on the garden table, she glanced at her phone. No messages from Rossiter today, but it was still early.

She'd thought long and hard about whether or not to go with Clarke to the Italian wedding. He was expecting her decision today, as he needed to book either one or two tickets. True to his word, he hadn't put any pressure on Ana to accept the offer, but time was of the essence, and decision day was looming. The trip had come up a couple of times in various conversations and texts over the last few days, but she had never felt as though he was trying to force her into joining him.

Her mother and friends' stance hadn't changed, however. They were still against the idea, but told Analisse that it was her decision to make, and hers alone.

After much deliberation and a few more contemplative sips of tea, she picked up her phone. The sun reflected off the screen into her eyes, momentarily dazzling her. She duly shielded them, scrolled through her contacts to find her former professor and lover's number, and dialled. After a few seconds, he answered:

"Hi Clarke. It's me. I ummm.... I have something to say."

Rossiter knew instinctively that Ana had reached a decision about the wedding. Her stuttering tone of voice wasn´t a good sign. He in turn felt nervous, as even though he was still bitterly disappointed that she would only ever want to be friends with him, he desperately wanted her to join him.

He cleared his throat, and attempting to regain a measure of composure, answered her:

"Miss Lejeune. I presume you´ve come to a decision vis à vis le wedding en Italie?"

"Yes, I have."

"Go on, just hit me with it, tell me straight. Yay or nay?"

Analisse took a deep breath, one that seemed like the deepest she´d ever taken. Exhaling, she announced to the still mildly panic-stricken Clarke:

"Sorrento, here we come! You´d better book those billets, Professor Rossiter!"

Clarke was so happy, excited and relieved, too. She´d had him going there, for a moment. He took a deep breath, cleared his throat, as was almost second nature to him now by virtue of having to raise his voice to be heard above scores of noisy students in the classroom, and spoke again to continue the conversation.

"That´s a very good answer, miss Lejeune! I´m delighted that we´ll be sampling tiramisu and tortellini together! We just need to have a brief chat before I book the tickets, to make sure that we get everything organised and that the arrangements are to your liking! Are you free tonight at seven?"

Analisse mentally consulted her diary to check that nothing was on the agenda, and with a contented smile, agreed to meet the professor that evening.

At the agreed time, Ana rang the doorbell of number fourteen Newbury Court. Rossiter opened the door and invited her inside with that trademark smile.

"Buonasera, bella! Come stai? Tutto bene?"

"Errrr... not too sure what that means, but I´ll hazard a guess at something resembling good evening or bonsoir?"

"Right you are! I haven´t got any Chianti to embrace the Italian theme, but can I interest you in one of your two favourite Ms: c´est à dire, Malibu or Mojito?"

Ana smirked as she casually discarded her jacket and made her way through the kitchen and headed outside to sit on the bandstand. Even though it wasn´t yet summer, the spring evening was still pleasantly warm, so she surmised that sitting outside wouldn´t be a problem.

"Malibu, please!" she called out to Clarke, making her way outside.

They spent the next two hours planning the trip to Sorrento, a place they´d both heard great things about, but one that neither of them had ever visited. To outsiders, the choice of the Amalfi coast for a wedding where neither bride nor groom were Italian, may have seemed a somewhat strange one. The reason for said choice was that Rossiter´s future sister-in-law, while hailing from Belfast, was of Italian descent. All of those Italian relatives were no longer alive, but Clarke´s younger brother and his fiancée had chosen Sorrento as the venue for the ceremony both to honour lost loved ones, and also because it had been the place where he had popped the question. Hence, the chic coastal town seemed a fitting place for them to tie the knot.

Analisse took a thoughtful sip of Malibu and smiled enquiringly in Clarke´s direction. She didn´t seem nervous or stressed, but it was almost as though there was something preoccupying her; the smile that she offered appeared to be one that intimated that she was seeking assurances of some kind. She looked down at her glass, and spoke hesitantly:

"Listen, Clarke. All this planning is exciting, and I can´t wait to go. But... what about hotels, sleeping arrangements? You told me about one you´d seen a few hours ago. But it´s a room with a double bed, and I think it´s better if we opt for two singles. It wouldn´t be a good idea for us to share a bed..."

There it was. A royal kick to the ball bag! The professor had half expected something like this to happen. Even though he and Ana had decided to give their complicated friendship another go, it was still something of a delicate situation. Clarke had found a hotel online that looked great, but if Analisse wasn´t comfortable with them sleeping in the same bed, he would have to rethink his plans.

"Ok, I get where you´re coming from. The most important thing is that you feel comfortable, wherever we choose to stay. But are you sure you won´t at least consider us staying there?"

"No. I´m sorry Clarke, but it´s just not happening", said Ana with a stern look.

Rossiter was disappointed, but it wasn´t the end of the world. Naturally, the idea of sharing a bed with Analisse Lejeune, especially in Italia, one of the most romantic and passionate countries in the world, would always be tempting to him. But if she wasn´t at ease with it, then they would stay in another hotel. He had found one that he´d put down as the second choice. It had two single beds instead of a double, but they were literally five centimetres apart. It was also more expensive, but finance wasn´t a problem. It just frustrated the professor somewhat that he would have to pay more for the sake of a few lousy centimetres!

In spite of this, Clarke, like Ana, was extremely excited at the prospect of going on a new adventure. He´d always enjoyed weddings, but to be going to such a spectacular place with a dazzling démoiselle on his arm threatened to make his imagination run wild. Yes, their bond was special, and their ´friendship` a complicated one, but however much Rossiter tried, he just couldn´t help getting his hopes up. Beni Rothwell had urged him just a few weeks previously to do everything in his power to persuade Ana to go with him. But the Frenchy had been very hesitant, and Clarke had thought it highly improbable that she would be joining him on the plane to Naples. But alas, she had surprisingly decided to do just that. They had another couple of drinks and Clarke booked the hotel, much to Ana´s satisfaction. Sorrento was sorted, and whatever happened next, it promised to be anything but boring...

29.

It was now the day of Analisse and Clarke's departure. The professor wearily rolled over in bed as he attempted to blow away the cobwebs. The previous night's somewhat excessive wine consumption had left Rossiter feeling a little worse for wear, but his decision to partake of more vino than usual was a means of trying to relax before the trip.

He was looking forward to going, but also unsure of exactly how the trip would pan out. One of his French friends, J.C. Foiré, was giving Clarke a lift to the airport, and the excitement was palpable. Rossiter had built lasting friendships with all of the boys he'd met during that fabled first year in France in the hallowed halls of the Sextellan university residence; J.C, Ollie Villou, Antonio D´Ambrosino being those with whom he'd forged the strongest links as they'd spent those unforgettable times in France's deep south. Those initial nine months as a teaching assistant in one of the town's secondary schools remained to this day Clarke's happiest times. They'd been neighbours in the *cité u*, living on the same corridor, where they'd indulged in countless soirées that had been the stuff of legend. It had been the best year of his entire life.

Clarke was snapped out of his reminiscing by the sound of J.C. wandering into the flat, banging the door against the wall, cigarette in hand. The French chainsmoker extraordinaire was incapable of ever doing anything quietly. Rossiter's mind went back to the numerous occasions over the years when his buddy had slept over on the couch after typically heavy drinking sessions. On such occasions, the first thing Clarke heard would be J.C. ambling around in the kitchen, banging cupboard doors at some ungodly hour without a care in the world, in pursuit of coffee to go with what was doubtless his fifteenth cigarette of the morning, déjà. Monsieur Foiré drank more coffee and smoked more cigarettes than anyone the professor had ever known. Hence, it was no surprise to see his friend contentedly puffing away on yet another *clope* as he entered the premises, unleashing a rasping fart as he did so.

"Ça va, Watson!", he bellowed as his arms stretched up above his head, light brown hair reflecting in the sunlight. Foiré always nicknamed the professor thus, given that almost every Frenchman was familiar with the name, seeing it as archetypally English. Whether such a comparison with Clarke was particularly accurate or deserved was open to debate, but the nickname amused Rossiter, nonetheless.

J.C. was tall and well – built, with a slight beer belly not unlike Rossiter´s, courtesy of a liking for the booze and a healthy appetite. Like Clarke, J.C. was a likeable and intelligent young man who enjoyed the simple things in life. Since they´d first met in the Sextellan all those years ago, the two had always got on well. J.C. was easy – going, friendly, loyal, and with a wicked sense of humour. Given that both of them were from humble backgrounds, they´d hit it off instantly. Stubbing out his cigarette and immediately fishing another one from his pocket, he motioned towards the door:

"We ought to get going. The airport run at this time of day can be the bordel, you know."

"Yeah, let´s hit the road!" Rossiter grabbed his jacket and suitcase and followed his French friend to the car. The journey to the airport was quicker than they´d anticipated. Upon arrival at Payday deux departures, J.C. helped Clarke with his bags as they waited for Analisse to arrive.

"You´re gonna have an amazing time! Weddings are always great fun, and from what you´ve told me, the girl you´re going with is cute!"

"That she is, my friend! I just hope everything goes as smoothly as possible. Drama never seems to be far away where Analisse is concerned!"

"Ah... c´est bon! Don´t worry, you´ll both have a brilliant time!" replied Foiré, smiling as he noticed a girl heading in their direction with a wave. He´d yet to meet Ana, but the young twenty-something moving towards them fitted the description given by Clarke on the numerous occasions that he´d talked about her to his French friends, so it had to be her.

Stumbling over to them and dragging a wheeled suitcase behind her, Analisse exhaled, red – faced but smiling, as she reached J.C. and Clarke.

"Bonjour!"

"Bonjour to you too, Ana! This is my friend from Fort de Bouc, J.C. Foiré. J.C. – I give you the one and only Analisse Lejeune!"

"Bonjour, Ana. Clarke ´as tell me almost everysing about you!", replied Foiré in his charming French drawl. Pleasantries were exchanged between the two newly – acquainted compatriots, before J.C. duly bade Analisse and Rossiter goodbye. Their Italian adventure was about to get underway!

Foiré drove away, pulling on yet another cigarette as he waved goodbye. Clarke smiled excitedly at her as they made their way to departures. The professor could tell that Analisse was looking forward to the trip too, but he also sensed a tension in her. To what it may have been owing, he had no idea. She wasn't a frequent flyer, and heading to foreign climes with a former teacher – to a wedding, no less – wasn't exactly what one might term an everyday occurrence. Hence, Rossiter put it down to Ana being nervous at the prospect of a step into the unknown; a fun but potentially fraught situation with a former lover.

The first of their two flights – they had a layover in Rome prior to arriving in Naples – passed off uneventfully. Rossiter debated having a drink or two, but decided against it, wanting to keep as clear a head as possible. He and Analisse spent the majority of the flight making plans for what they would do upon arrival. They were both excited – that much was clear – but he still sensed that she was distant, distracted somehow.
Was there more to this than met the eye? Only time would tell...

After a fitful few minutes' sleep, Clarke was awoken abruptly by the captain's voice announcing their imminent descent into Rome. Rossiter stifled a yawn and attempted to rouse himself, before turning to Ana:

"Stage one of the journey's almost complete! It's a pain in the arse that we've got to spend four hours in the capital en route to Napoli, but not to worry!"

"Yeah, not ideal, mais c'est pas grave", replied Ana.

A few minutes later, they landed in Rome. After making sure that they'd left nothing behind, and waited for all the other passengers to disembark, Ana and Clarke were ready to go. Rossiter had to wait for his pre-booked disability assistance to arrive. The professor always organised this whenever he flew anywhere. He was fine travelling alone, and highly independent in general, but he preferred to reserve help getting through airports and on and off planes; it made life easier when in transit. Analisse however, hadn't done likewise. She hated drawing any attention to her own disability; in fact, it was almost as though she were in denial of its very existence at times. She'd insisted to Clarke that she wouldn't be wanting or needing any assistance whatsoever, but that she was more than happy for Clarke to take up the option, if he so chose. Shortly afterwards, they were greeted by two Romans in florescent yellow vests, who assisted them to the front of the aircraft and down the steps. Rossiter drew on the extremely basic Italian he'd learned during his university days in an attempt to make polite conversation with the two gentlemen, succeeding in making himself understood, though little else. His endeavours were greeted with a smile, which he found rewarding. When travelling to a new country, Clarke always attempted to learn something in the native tongue, even if only a few words. It was polite, and showed a willingness to embrace new cultures and experiences, which he believed to be important. Clarke had always enjoyed languages, so travelling allowed him to indulge one of his true passions, with varying degrees of success.

 Having arrived at the terminal, Ana and Clarke now had a four-hour wait until their flight to Naples. After going through all the usual airport rigmarole, they found a place to sit down. Almost immediately after they'd done so, Analisse's phone beeped for the third or fourth time in the few minutes since they'd arrived in the capital. She giggled contentedly, turning away from Clarke to make sure that he couldn't see her phone screen as she typed a response with a beaming smile etched upon her satisfied face. After Ana had finished typing and put the phone back into her pocket, Clarke turned back to her.

"Your phone's been beeping almost non-stop since we landed. You youngsters with all these phones and gadgets you've got nowadays. I can't keep track anymore."

Ana looked hesitantly back at him, before speaking with a note of caution:

"Listen, Clarke, there's something I need to tell you..."

Rossiter had the uneasy feeling that there was a guy involved. The almost incessant beeping, and the delighted smile that had been on Analisse's face ever since they'd landed, didn't make it too difficult to put the pieces together. Clarke looked her directly in the eye.

"Yes? What is it?", he probed, with Ana now looking increasingly nervous.

"Those messages were off a guy from uni. We've been getting on well in class lately, and he says he wants to be with me. We're not together, and nothing has happened yet... and I'm not even sure if anything will... but I prefer to be honest with you."

Absolutely fucking terrific!

Although Ana's revelation had been somewhat expected, the feeling of frustration and disappointment weighed upon the professor, almost suffocating him. In fact, it was more than that; his dejection was bordering on anger. Here they were, all set for what was supposed to be the trip of a lifetime. Clarke was still hoping that old sparks might be reignited, romance reborn; people were always happy and often horny at weddings, and the professor had been hoping that the Amalfi coast, with its sun dappled shorelines and an ambience of matrimonial merriment, might just pave the way for he and Analisse to get back on track. But this bolt from the blue was like a kick in the cojones to Rossiter, and any hopes of Prosecco-fuelled passion setting their Sorrento hotel room ablaze had now been unceremoniously extinguished, resembling nothing more than the dying embers of a love story that was soon to be confined to the past and snuffed out, never to be rekindled.

Clarke was feeling incredibly annoyed and disappointed with the news of Analisse's new suitor. But after a few minutes' reflection, he decided that the best way to deal with it was to block it out and concentrate on enjoying what nevertheless promised to be an amazing few days with a girl who still meant a great deal to him. He would make sure that they enjoyed the trip as much as possible, regardless of any *new kid on the block* who fancied his chances of wooing her. He and Ana hadn't spoken in the few minutes following what she'd told him. But now feeling more relaxed, he turned to her:

"I can't say this latest revelation hasn't come as something of a disappointment. But let's just enjoy the trip, ok? I just want to make the most of it, and not worry about anything else. What do you say?" Rossiter's eyes were fixed intently upon Ana, as though probing for a response. Her reply was direct and to the point:

"Listen, Clarke, I've already been very clear about the fact that nothing – absolutely nothing – will happen between us on this trip. I've only ever seen it as an opportunity to spend a few days in a beautiful place, with a *friend*. Nothing more."

So, that was that. Rossiter's hopes of another limoncello – soaked *liaison dangereuse* were well and truly dashed. It was time to forget about it.

"Sure, no problem. Let's just enjoy ourselves!" he said, before turning away and resting his eyes. He knew he wouldn't be able to sleep – especially in such noisy surroundings as an airport – but they still had hours to kill before their flight to Naples. Rossiter rested and read for a while, until it was eventually time to go.

The departure lounge speaker system announced that their flight would soon be boarding. Clarke and Analisse gathered up their hand luggage and headed for the gate. After a short time waiting in the queue, they showed their passports and boarding passes, and accompanied once again by disability assistance staff, Rossiter and his scrumptious accomplice climbed the aircraft steps and got to their seats ready for take-off. Surprisingly, they both slept for the majority of the flight, and Rossiter was both startled and thirsty upon being awoken by the news that they would soon be landing in old Napoli. The descent took a little over ten minutes, during which, due to the incessant popping of her ears, Ana asked Clarke whether he had anything that she could suck.
Ooh la la!

After some turbulence and a somewhat shaky landing – perhaps a metaphor for the professor and Analisse's relationship – they took their bags from the overhead lockers and prepared to disembark for the second time that day. Rossiter's florescent - jacketed assistants duly arrived, with miss Lejeune almost snarling at them as they offered to take her bags too.

She refused with an irritated wave of the hand, and they walked down the steps towards the baggage reclaim hall. After a brief wait to pick up their suitcases off the conveyor belt, Clarke and Ana followed the signs in search of the bus to Sorrento. Having stowed their luggage, they sat down in readiness for the two-hour journey. It was early evening and still warm, which prompted a thirsty Rossiter to order a beer. He was surprised that alcohol should be available on a bus, but the icy cold beverage went down a treat and went some way to reinvigorating him, in what was an unexpectedly pleasant start to the holiday.

    The professor sipped on more beers as the bus wound through the hilltop roads, with plush green trees and beautifully colourful flowers providing a vibrant backdrop beneath a dazzling blue sky; the scenery on this part of the Amalfi coast was nothing short of exquisite. It was a relaxing journey, and they arrived in Sorrento after a little over two hours on the road. After dropping other passengers off at various places across town, Ana and Clarke eventually arrived at their hotel as dusk set in, wrestling the waning light from the sky as day succumbed to night. It was a strange building of bright pink walls, with Mount Vesuvius in the background, the nocturnal evening waves caressing the sand as the evening drew in. Neither Rossiter nor Analisse had ever seen a pink hotel before; it seemed unusual, but welcoming, nonetheless. They checked in, and promptly took their luggage up to the room.

  "Well, here we are, Ana!" said Clarke, collapsing onto the bed and stretching out, satisfied.

  "Yeah! It's going to be great! I'm glad we're finally here!" replied Ana, with a contented smile.

"Do you feel like heading out for a drink or two and seeing what this place is all about?"

"Okay, sure, why not!"

They showered quickly, and went to meet Rossiter's mother and stepfather, Linda and Tray, who had arrived a few days earlier along with Clarke's aunt and uncle. That first evening in Italy was hugely enjoyable, as were the ones that followed.

The whole trip transpired to be as incredible as Rossiter had hoped for, and much more besides. The only slight disappointment for Clarke had been a rain – soaked yet still enjoyable day trip to Amalfi, where he had wanted to go in order to visualise the remarkable city where one of his high school English Literature exam texts had been set. He and Analisse had made the most of the opportunities that Sorrento and the surrounding area had presented to them, with pizza, pasta and gelato aplenty. They'd had a truly wonderful time, and were now approaching the end of the final evening of their stay. Having eaten more Italian finery than either Clarke or Analisse had ever thought possible, they had one final repast and headed back to the hotel. There had been intermittent bouts of stress from Analisse throughout the trip, as she battled with the conflict of being in this wonderful part of the world with Rossiter, coupled with her growing desire to take things further with her university classmate, whose flurry of text messages while they'd been waiting at the airport in Rome had rather put the kibosh on the professor's hopes of *doing the nasty before the antipasti.*

As they got back to the room, however, Ana was in jovial mood. She nonchalantly slung her handbag onto a nearby chair, and sat down on the bed, still full after the final pizza of their stay and a considerable amount of wine. She´d been more than a little hesitant to go on the trip with the man who had once been her professor, but she had to acknowledge that despite a few stressful moments, it had been a fantastic experience. Clarke had promised her the holiday of a lifetime, and neither he nor the jaw – droppingly beautiful Amalfi coast, with its sumptuous food, vino and breathtaking scenery, had disappointed. True to his word, Rossiter had treated Ana not merely like a Duchess of Amalfi, but a princess or queen. She had paid for absolutely nothing during their entire stay, with the exception of a single round of drinks. He had insisted upon paying for everything, so who was she to argue?

  As she sat down on the corner of the bed, the Limoncello hit Ana hard. She´d had a few tipsy moments as a teenager, but she was slowly beginning to realise that this was the first time that she´d felt *drunk*. She wasn´t hammered, merely contented and intent on enjoying her final night with Rossiter in this truly wonderful setting. Clarke got up and wandered to the bathroom. He was drunk too, but this wasn´t new territory for him. He closed the bathroom door and began to relieve himself, but nothing could have prepared him for what happened next. A laugh, almost a shriek so shrill was its nature, emanated from the bedroom. Ana was apparently fully under the influence of the lethal Limoncello, laughing uncontrollably as the professor zipped up and made his way out of the bathroom. He wondered what was going on:

"Ahhhhh! Claaaaaarke! The room´s spinning! The lightshade is going to fall on me!"

Rossiter's beaming grin broke out into full on laughter as he made his way toward the bed and sat down next to Ana.

"Haha! Don't worry, Ana! Nothing's going to fall on you! You just made the mistake of mixing wine and Limoncello. A word to the wise: never mix drinks. That's a schoolboy – or indeed schoolgirl – error! But fear not, ma lady; ever the professor, I will educate you on the perilous faux pas of the unenlightened drinker!"

Analisse stretched out on the bed, a smile returning to her lips as all thoughts of falling lightshades and the impending abyss left her. She was now drunk – more than *pompette* – and she would doubtless pay the price tomorrow morning. They were due to fly home early, and she'd never had a hangover before. That was yet another dubious honour to be bestowed upon Professor Rossiter.

Say whatever you like about Clarke: he had promised Ana a memorable holiday, and he hadn't disappointed. The inevitable *gueule de bois* would be tough, but Analisse had experienced a holiday like no other. As she clumsily undressed and rolled over to sleep, she was well aware that whatever the future held for her and Clarke, it would never be boring. He gave her a gentle kiss on the forehead and bade her goodnight. Rossiter was a lot of things; a complicated character in some respects and yet remarkably simple in others, but she knew how much he loved and cared for her. Nothing else mattered.

30.

The following morning's hangover was predictably brutal. Being considerably more accustomed to the perils of the demon drink, the battle – hardened Rossiter rolled tiredly yet nonchalantly out of bed and shuffled to the bathroom to pee, before calling out to Ana, who was still dead to the world:

"Miss Lejeune! Rouse yourself! The bus to Napoli waits for no man – or woman – for that matter!"

It was insanely early. It had only just turned 5 am, with Sorrento and nearby Mount Vesuvius – resplendent in its early morning volcanic slumber – a joy to behold from the hotel room window. Both Clarke and Ana would've preferred to have booked flights at a more convenient time – that went without saying – but the professor had already succumbed to Ana's insistence on booking a room with single beds – and more expensive to boot – which meant that their choice of flights had unfortunately been limited to the early morning. After having taken a shower, Clarke called out to Analisse again, and she finally emerged from beneath the duvet in disgruntled fashion, hurriedly brushing her immaculate ivories and heading for a shower, before emerging, still somewhat befuddled, and throwing on the clothes that she'd laid outside her suitcase the night before in a fit of Limoncello – fuelled lethargy.

"Bloody 'ell! It's soooo early!"

"Yes, it is. But we need to get going, pronto!"

Analisse almost grimaced as she cast a fatigued glance in Clarke's direction, instantly regretting the previous evening's not inconsiderable alcohol consumption. If this was what hangovers were like, they were nothing to write home about.

She took a few minutes to gather her thoughts and her things, and with head throbbing, followed Clarke out of their room. They checked out of the hotel, said farewell to Sorrento and hailed a taxi to Naples airport. Ana managed to get a few minutes' sleep during the two-hour journey, but it was largely insufficient, as the hangover was proving irrepressible. When they'd eventually arrived at the airport, checked in their luggage and waited for what seemed an eternity to board their connecting flight to Brussels Charleroi – an airport and city that turned out to be as grey and soulless as the depressing, slate coloured sky that hung above them – Clarke turned to Ana:

"How's the head? Hangovers can be a challenge, even at the best of times. But when you add in the fact that this is your first experience of the much beguiled *gueule de bois* – and that we got up at stupid o'clock, to boot – I totally understand your suffering!"

Ana looked back at Clarke, still feeling awful.

"I've never felt this bad in my whole life! Why do people put themselves through this, some on a regular basis? I just feel as though I want the ground to swallow me up, or something!"

"Yes, never pleasant, and hangovers certainly don't get any easier with age. Take it from someone who knows!"

Rossiter cast a sympathetic glance Analisse's way and fastened his seat belt ready for take-off. Needless to say, mademoiselle had continued to feel the effects of the previous night's Limoncello throughout the first flight to Belgium and the second one back home. She tried in vain to sleep, and once they finally arrived at her house having landed and then retrieved their luggage, Ana wasted little time in collapsing on her bed, almost forgetting to even acknowledge Clarke as he prepared to walk back home, looking somewhat forlorn as he opened Ana's front door to leave.

"Right, well, I guess that's that, then."
Analisse, slumped on her bed and apparently in no mood for small talk, bade farewell to the professor with a dismissive wave of the hand.

"Sorry Clarke. I'm just feeling so tired and ill right now. Thank you for a great holiday. I'll be in touch when I'm feeling a little bit more alive. Ok? See you."

Rossiter nodded curtly in response and walked home briskly, more than a little irritated by Analisse's total disregard for his feelings, of which the overriding one was regret. Yes, Sorrento had been a memorable experience, but not for the reasons he might have expected. As he turned into Newbury Court and headed up the drive of number fourteen, Clarke was well aware that the Italian sojourn marked the end of this particular chapter in his and Analisse Lejeune's story. But it was potentially more than that: perhaps this was the *end* of the story, full stop.

31.

As the professor opened the front door and wandered somewhat bemusedly across the threshold of the hallowed number fourteen Newbury Court, it was safe to say that the brain cogs were whirring.

Of course, he was disappointed that Sorrento had yielded little more than mere pizza and pleasantries, rather than the much hoped for bouts of soul bearing and clothes tearing. But alas, this was the end of the latest chapter in Rossiter and Analisse's tumultuous tale, and there could be no turning back.

In a vain attempt to banish any lingering thoughts of the luscious miss Lejeune from his mind, Clarke wandered distractedly into the kitchen to select a drink over which to meditate and plot his next move. He chose a beer, which was admittedly boring, but he had a raging thirst, and needed to calm it as soon as possible.

Distractedly scanning the living room, he noted that the place was in desperate need of a spring clean. But he'd never been one for housekeeping; the prospect of attacking the lino with mop and bucket held no appeal whatsoever. As he sat and pondered the events of the last few days, he decided that any cleaning would have to wait.

Slumping onto the sofa, Clarke, perhaps for the first time in his entire life, reluctantly acknowledged that this situation with Analisse was – to put it bluntly – a fight that he simply couldn't win. The more Rossiter ruminated on the situation, the word *fight* was somewhat moot, at this point. Yes, he and Ana had had more than their fair share of ups and downs, more than a sprinkling of tempestuous moments. But as their story had unfolded, Clarke was forced to acknowledge that, for all the difficult times, this had been a part of his life that had nevertheless provided him with countless unforgettable experiences and lessons to be learned. He and miss Lejeune were undoubtedly complex characters – perhaps more so than he had initially realised – but they were alike in some ways, too. Perhaps that was the very reason why things between them had never been as one might have expected.

Food for thought, indeed...

After one more drink, the professor lethargically lifted himself from his slumber and made for the bedroom. He would be sleeping alone tonight – and not for the first time in his life – but tomorrow was another day, and life sans Analisse was something he needed to start getting used to. Sooner or later, his chagrin would pass, and the prospect of a Frenchy-free future would undoubtedly be an unusual yet enticing one...

Epilogue

Clarke tossed and turned irritably as the early morning Spanish sun peeped through the window blinds in an overly exuberant attempt to wake him. Said shutter had only recently been repaired by his new Italian friend who went by the name of Gianluca Brutusini – a newly qualified engineer from Naples that Rossiter had been introduced to by his colleague – and Brutusini's girlfriend – a Greek / German girl by the name of Marie Finesse.

They were a truly lovely couple and had become dear friends in recent times. Gianluca had offered to lend a hand when the shutters in the professor's apartment had given up the proverbial ghost, and Clarke had been eternally grateful to his friend for having been able to fix them. But as the sun unashamedly crept through the tired wooden slats, he couldn't help wishing for a few extra minutes of shut-eye.

      Several months had passed since Sorrento. Clarke had kept in touch with Ana for the first few weeks after they had returned from Italy, and they still exchanged occasional messages, but correspondence had subsequently become less and less frequent with every passing week. Their relationship – if one could call it that – was much less strained than it had been a few months previously. They continued to exchange pleasantries, but little more. The last he had heard, Ana was teaching English in a small town in her native France. If what had existed between Clarke and

Analisse had once been something of an emotional minefield, it could now merely be termed little more than *textual intercourse*.

The professor looked tiredly at the clock. It was only just after seven. Despite desperately wanting to go back to sleep, he reluctantly got out of bed, went to the bathroom, and did his best to prepare for what would doubtless be another big day. In the aftermath of everything that had happened with Analisse, Rossiter had made the momentous decision to leave Congletown and move to Spain. He'd felt that a change of scenery, culture and language would do him good. His Spanish was still something of what one might politely term *a work in progress*, but he was making headway, and it was proving to be a hugely enjoyable experience thus far.

Rossiter had found a job at a Spanish language school and was also teaching English to Russians for another company online. Remote working had now become commonplace in the aftermath of the Novid-19 pandemic, which suited Clarke down to the ground, as he was now able to spend the majority of the week working from home. Salaries for teachers in Spain were notoriously low, but he had been well aware of that before having chosen to depart for pastures new. He had been forced to combine the two jobs in order to make ends meet, but his hours were flexible, which allowed him plenty of free time to enjoy the Spanish sun, palm trees, and scores of sexy señoritas whom he encountered on a daily basis. Despite a tumultuous few months, Clarke considered himself a man of simple pleasures. He had built a wonderfully fulfilling life for himself in his new surroundings, as he had done previously in both Congletown and France. For as much as he enjoyed his work the majority of the time, it was still a means to an end; a way of paying the bills, and little more. Even though he was now living in his third different country and approaching his fortieth year, work still wasn't high on Clarke Rossiter's list of priorities. He was professional, and did any job to the best of his ability. But any incumbent stress – or lack thereof – would never be his primary concern, and these jobs were no different.

 The professor turned on his laptop and logged into various teaching platforms, as per his relatively new daily routine. He sipped a café con leche as he read through a welcomingly sparse spread of emails, feeling only mildly irritated as he stumbled through an almost incoherent request from his boss at the Spanish school to compile student reports before the end of the academic year, which was fast approaching.

 The day went quickly, as did the rest of the week. Compared to the other jobs he'd done in his twenties and early thirties, Rossiter's new Spanish life was a cinch. He had plenty of free time, and he also continued to watch his beloved Fort Dale Football Club from afar. He had even given himself time off work in order to travel home to Congletown to see them win the playoff final at the national stadium and be promoted to the league above. Making the trip with his mother, younger brother and nephew, it had been a glorious experience, and a day of celebration. Even though it was only football, it had been one of the happiest days in Clarke Rossiter's life.

 With the weekend now in full swing, the professor lit his customary Sunday cigar, leaning back to take in the afternoon sunshine on his balcony as the palm trees swayed in the breeze. Rossiter inhaled, subsequently blowing out a smoke ring to accompany the bourbon that he nonchalantly sipped. As the early summer sun beat down, Clarke thought about just how wonderful and care-free of a new life he had made for himself in the wonderful city of Valencia. He had his friends, hobbies, and a harem of hotties whenever he pleased. This was *la dolce vita*, and Analisse Lejeune seemed a world away.

Rossiter put his cigar in the ashtray and headed for the bathroom. The Spanish sun was enticing him to drink more beer than usual, and as such, he regularly needed to pee. The professor finished, grabbed another cold can from the fridge, and headed back out onto the balcony. He really enjoyed sitting out there, the only drawback being that it backed onto an extremely busy road.

Clarke leaned back in the sunshine and took another sip of beer, then bourbon. Amid the crescendo of car horns blaring out through the baking hot afternoon sky, it was the comparably subdued beep of his phone that caught Rossiter by surprise, somewhat.

The professor rarely looked at his phone at the weekend, but he was expecting a message from a cute German blonde he´d been messaging for the last few days, so thought it best to have a look. But it wasn´t from her. This text was from an all too familiar source:

"Hi Clarke. We need to talk. This can´t wait..."

Printed in Great Britain
by Amazon